The Flawed

The Flawed

PAUL DUNN

The Flawed

Copyright ©2021 Paul Dunn

All rights reserved. No part of this publication may be reproduced, stored in or introduced into a retrieval system, or transmitted in any form, or by any means, without the prior written permission of the author.

Edited by Christine Driver (CleverEditors.com)
Cover design by Stephanie Dunn
Book design by David W. Edelstein

ISBN:
978-0-9687460-6-6 (hardcover)
978-0-9687460-3-5 (paperback)
978-0-9687460-4-2 (ebook)

TheFlawed.ca

Contents

Introduction *1*

1. Our Struggle *5*

2. The Giver of Lies' Mansion *12*

3. The Mission *19*

4. The Long Journey Back Home *36*

5. The Spy Mission *55*

6. The Journey to Mount Hemor *63*

7. Fighting for Freedom *81*

8. We Are Going Home *91*

9. Shooting Stars *107*

10. Too Many Elds *135*

11. The Alien Base *150*

12. The Fight of Our Lives *167*

13. The Final Battle *175*

Epilogue *191*

The Flawed

INTRODUCTION

ON THE OUTER EDGES OF THE PLANETARY SYSTEM, amongst millions of stars and galaxies, there is a small planet called Ashan. It is a planet much like Earth, with similar attributes like water, air, and four changing seasons. On the southern hemisphere of Ashan, there is a continent called Derbe. In the middle of Derbe is a large forest. In that forest, there lives a people called the Flawed, the Flawed called the land where they live the Solar Complex. They have lived there for generations. They work and help each other—they live peaceful lives. Some are farmers, carpenters, and some own small businesses—hardware shops, a small school, a library and a few ma' and pa' corner stores. There is only one blacksmith. At the end of the day, for each of them, life comes down to raising children and being neighbourly. You could say they are a close community.

But somewhere along the way, something big

happened that changed life in all the Solar Complex, and it affected many of us. It was not talked about very much, but now and then some of the older Flawed would speak of how life used to be, not so long ago. My name is Jenny, and I have witnessed the struggles in our daily life from what has happened to us and how it has affected my family. I see the effects on their minds and the many ways they try to cope. It is heartbreaking to watch somebody you have known and loved for a long time decline into the depths of forgetfulness, to the point where they gradually forget your name and the things that were once most important to them.

I remember, not so long ago, listening to an older gentleman called Hopkins. He would reminisce about the blue sky and the fields of green, and he would talk about the rivers—of how he used to fish in them.

"And the water," he said expressively, as he held his hands above his head, saying, "It was so clean, you could drink from it! Do you remember that?" asked Hopkins, as he nudged his friend who sat alongside him. His friend said nothing but continued to stare off in the distance. He resumed talking and said, "Life was particularly good, until things started to go bad." He stopped talking, I noticed a tear come from his eye. Then he was off in the distance once more, his train of thought was gone. You could see he was dreaming of better days.

Then another old soul piped up. His name was Abner. Now and then he would speak out loud and say, "I want to go fishing," or "I would like to take a walk in the woods, and smell the flowers, and walk along the green mossy path by the peaceful rippling river. I remember how it used to be," Abner mumbled to himself, and then he stopped talking about it too. But for a moment, he and Hopkins did remember how it used to be, but only for those few moments, and then it was gone.

"Poor Abner," replied Hopkins.

All I can say is that nobody knew for sure what happened. Some said it was just an old folk tale, passed down from generation to generation. Some of the older Flawed who have long since gone called it the "Darkness". At times, they would remember the little things, but their memory was failing, and there was nothing anyone could do. But one thing was known for sure—something was wrong in all the Solar Complex. I have overheard the older Flawed say the sky is not so blue as it used to be, and the grass is not so green, and the rivers and the lakes have gone dark, and the fish have disappeared along with the flowers. But life continues from day to day.

I have heard some others say that in the early stages of the Darkness, it was like the feeling of forgetfulness. Like you forgot where you had placed something—you go to find it and it is gone, but where can it be? You cannot remember. It was a mental thing, and it was confusing. It affected the Flawed in different ways, but that is the one thing known by all the Flawed. So, they continued the struggle, in the daily grind of coping in the Solar Complex.

But, through all the confusion and the forgetfulness, the Flawed had hope, and that hope was in their children, whom they called the "young ones." The young ones, it seemed, had escaped the Darkness, the confusion, and the forgetfulness. For, when they were under the age of six, some of them would have a clear vision and had seen and spoken of things to come, and that had encouraged the Flawed over time. But, at the age of seven, some of the young ones would succumb to the darkness, and the visions were gone forever. Then they would begin to feel the early signs of being different—misplacing things, forgetfulness. But the Flawed knew their future was in their young ones, and they continued having young ones with the hope that someday soon, or a day far off in the future, one of them may get the clear vision and instructions that would lead them out of the Darkness in the Solar Complex.

This is how we live. It is painful, watching the older ones lose their minds and their real sense of being. I love this village and its people. It is who I am. I was, for the most part, an observer and sometimes a helper in these events—I wrote down what had happened to us—I am one of many, whom they called "the Flawed." Here is our story.

1

OUR STRUGGLE

IT WAS BY HAPPENSTANCE ONE DAY, OR SHOULD I say a sheer miracle, that one of the Flawed named Allicin, a young woman who worked at the Mayor's office as a clerk while researching the history of the local library, discovered in the archives a newspaper article that read, "Prosperity and a Bright Future for the Solar Complex." That caught Allicin's attention, and she began to read. The photo in the article showed a tall figure standing by the side of the senior members of the Solar Complex. Allicin who knew immediately who the tall figure was.

His name was Aldo Baca, but we know him now as the "Giver of Lies". We all call him the "GOL". He was an alien type of figure and about seven feet tall—a skeleton of a creature, with a gangly walk—and nobody knew for sure just where he came from. Of a kind nature he was not, and most of the Flawed feared him. Thinking about him and the article, Allicin pondered for a moment and then continued reading. The main part of the article stated that the Solar Complex was rich in minerals and that an agreement was signed by the hierarchy, giving rights to mine and extract such minerals. The GOL was in control, because he had convinced the community he was an expert in the field of geology.

The article went on to say the GOL had privately mined and developed a small area of land, and there he had discovered a huge deposit of silver. The GOL had given some of the members of the hierarchy and the community a portion of silver equal to a month's wages and the recipients were elated. And so the Giver of Lies had convinced them he could provide portions of silver every month for years to come. Celebrations had commenced, and the people in the Solar Complex figured that they had it made financially. So, the GOL convinced the senior members and the community to give him full rights to the minerals of the Solar Complex. Allicin sat back in her chair after reading the article with wonderment and awe, and she thought to herself, this is something worth looking into.

She looked for more articles and soon discovered that two weeks after the signing of the mineral contract, a severe solar storm which lasted two days wreaked havoc over the whole Solar Complex.

The curiosity and excitement of the newfound

information invigorated her, and she continued digging and reading more articles. She came across another one which read, "Change has Come to the Solar Complex." It went on to say that shortly after the solar storm—within days—most of the community had symptoms of dementia and a change in the land had occurred. The article said the solar storm was to blame for the recent activity and the change in the land. The sky was not so blue, and the grass was not so green—they were fading—the water turned dark, many of the fish had disappeared, and the flowers were fading.

"That's it!" she said, as she sat back in her chair and said, "That GOL fooled us all." She had put it all together. The years of confusion and the GOL— how he used the solar storm—but how did he do it? She did not know. Her mind was racing, and she was thinking, "I have to tell the members of the council, and I have to get this out."

She knew she was onto something and came across another article and began reading intently. Then the door of the archives opened with a creak. She heard it and said, "Who is there?" She quickly closed the article and listened. She could hear steps coming towards her, then, lo and behold, standing before her was the GOL himself.

He said, "I see you found something, Allicin," in his cynical voice.

"Yes," Allicin said, "I found it all!"

"That's too bad," he said.

"Why??" She trembled, suddenly afraid.

"It's simple—I want it all! It is just who I am. I cannot help it. It's my nature, and that's too bad for you." He said to her, "I have fooled your race for some time now, and I have made your people walk around in a daze for years and years. And you have no clue what I did, and that will be my little secret forever." He laughed most scornfully. Allicin got up and tried to escape, but he caught her, and in the struggle, he took her life.

The GOL removed the archived articles about himself and the mining of the land, and there was no more evidence or even a trace to let people know what had happened. He disappeared through the front door of the archives.

After about ten minutes of being terrified of what I had seen, I finally came out from the small room where I had peeked through the doorway and watched it all. I said nothing, because I was too frightened, but I did send a short note to let the council know where Allicin was.

Meanwhile, in the Solar Complex, a drawing from one of the young ones was discovered. It showed a bright image in the sky and read, "He is coming." An emergency meeting was called, and the council gathered to discuss the new vision and the drawing.

"It's been a long time since we have seen or heard of a vision from the young ones."

Lars the senior council member added, "All we can say is someone, somewhere has seen our plight and has sent us a message. He continued, "Please check daily on the young ones to see if there are further updates." After that, the birth rate in the Solar Complex increased greatly, even more so than it was before, for the Flawed figured if they have more young ones then they will have a better chance of receiving visions more frequently.

The GOL had found out about the drawing, the visions, and the council meeting through the excitement and a rumor that was spread around town of the good news. He was terribly upset and angry, and he left the Solar Complex for a couple of weeks. Shortly after, some of the older members of the council and the community lost their memory, and slight dementia had come to the middle-aged Flawed. Darkness, it seemed, increased slightly, and they felt it.

The Solar Complex was in a state of confusion, and people were very perplexed. They said daily to each other, "what is happening?" They did not know.

Another one of the council members, named Alban, had an opinion and said, "This never happened until the GOL went away. Now we have this," as he held up his hands in frustration and said, "this is maddening to our minds." They agreed collectively, and Alban continued, "We have to find out where this character went." Then Lars called for another meeting to discuss the growing Darkness and to find out what the GOL had done and where he'd gone.

The meeting was called, and only the elected members were privy to the information. In the meeting, all agreed that something must be done to the GOL. "What can we do?" asked Alban.

Lars spoke up, "Things have changed, and now we find ourselves in this predicament."

Another elected member said, "Not all of us have been affected by this, we still have good men and women. We have lived in fear of this character for a long time. First," he said, "We must find out where he lives. I am suggesting we put a tail on him—you know—follow him, until he leads us to his residence. Then we wait for the opportune time to break in and see what we can find out."

Alban continued and said, "This will get ugly extremely fast, and we are not prepared for a fight against him. We are ordinary men and women."

"Look!" said Lars, "Do you see what is happening? We are slowly dying, and we have to find out what is going on here in our village and other places in the Solar Complex."

"What do you suggest?" asked Alban.

Lars stood up and said, "I say, we secretly get our blacksmith ready to start producing weapons for the just-in-case measure, because who knows what this guy will do next."

"What will we tell him when he finds out about the activity at the foundry?" replied Alban.

"Just say we are making a few improvements to our infrastructure," said Lars.

"But we will have to hide all the weaponry," said Alban.

"Yes, that will be a problem," replied Lars

"I say we hide the weapons in our root cellars—he will never check there," said Alban.

"Okay, then," said Lars. "Are we all in agreement?"

"Yes," they said. They discussed the mission of spying on the GOL, and they selected both a qualified woman and a man. The blacksmith was ordered to fire up the foundry to get ready for the just-in-case scenario: war.

2

THE GIVER OF
LIES' MANSION

THE TWO SPIES WERE INSTRUCTED ON THEIR MIS-
sion and what was involved. When the right time presented itself, they followed the GOL incognito—he
never suspected a thing. They found out where he
lived. It was a huge mansion, fifty miles outside of the
Solar Complex. The two spies returned to the council
with a full report of his comings and goings. They
made a plan and waited for the opportune time to
move in and storm his house to see if they could find
something unusual or any useful clues.

The time came, and the hand-picked group of men
and women from the community and the council were
ready for the mission. According to their detailed plan,
they found the GOL's itinerary. He was going on a
trip to another country for a week.

No sooner had the GOL left his home than it was invaded by the search team. There were two guards on duty dressed in full covered face armour at the GOL's mansion, but they were easily removed. After they breached the mansion, the team left no stone unturned. They searched every nook and cranny of his elaborate home but had difficulty locating meaningful information. They were at their wit's end, searching high and low, saying to themselves, "There has to be something hidden here," and "think!" They said, "Where would somebody hide something valuable?" The team searched behind every picture and painting on the walls. But they found nothing.

Then, Lars was admiring one of the bookshelves and noticed an odd-looking book. He pulled out the book, and the bookshelf swung open to reveal another door. He called out for everybody to come. "I have found something." They all rushed to the small room and there, behind the hidden door, was a bank of drawers.

Lars quickly opened and searched all the drawers. He found a set of keys and an old, tattered, brown leather notebook with a leather string wrapped around it. "Funny looking keys, indeed," he remarked. As for the book, he unwrapped the leather string and opened it slowly. After turning a few pages, he discovered it contained a map to a land that was a seven-day journey away.

Lars turned another page, and he could not believe his eyes. The heading read "The Secret Book of Knowledge awaits." He turned to another page and read "How to be Unflawed."

"This is it!" he said in excitement.

"What's on the next page?" someone asked. Lars turned the page, and it showed a drawing of a cave by a giant oak tree, and the image of The Book of Secret Knowledge was imprinted over the opening.

"We struck gold!" Lars said, as he held the book in his hands. "Quickly, let's get this book and the keys back to the council to study them further."

When the council studied the book and keys, they determined that "The Secret Book of Knowledge" must be brought and united with the book called "How to be Unflawed", which was inside a cave at Mount Hemor, according to the drawing, a seven-day journey away.

"This journey has got to be made," said Lars. "Upon further investigation, before we make the trip to Mount Hemor, we have to acquire "The Secret Book of Knowledge." Our future depends upon this mission—we cannot go on dealing with this insanity any longer. We must take action against this tyranny that hinders our people!" exclaimed Lars.

Alban spoke up and said, "We have a problem."

"Yes," said Lars, "I know what you are going to say..."

Alban went on, "Where is this cave by the tall oak tree?"

"Yes," said Lars, "I was thinking about that. We have the map to Mount Hemor but nothing for this cave."

Alban said, "I know a local hunter called Darius. I wonder if he has seen this cave while on his recent hunting trip?"

"I will ask him," said Lars. "If anyone knows, it would be Darius." Lars took the book, concealed it in his pocket, and went to see the hunter.

Lars walked to where Darius lived and knocked on the door. Darius answered the door and said, "Lars, come on in! What is on your mind?"

Lars replied, "We raided the GOL's mansion and found a book in a secret hiding place. We have been studying it for a little while now," and as Lars was talking, he pulled out the book and opened it to the page with the drawing of a cave by the tall oak tree. He went on, "We are wondering if you know where this cave is located?"

Darius looked at the picture for a moment, and then it came to him. "Yes," He said. "I've slept there on hunting trips when it rained. But it is a seven-day journey from here."

"Great," said Lars. He gasped a little and said "I am so relieved you know where this place is."

Darius thumbed through the rest of the book and

saw the other drawings. He asked out of curiosity, "What is this all about, anyway?"

Lars said, "I think we have found out why we have been downtrodden all these years..."

"Yes," said Darius. "I saw a page that said 'How to be Unflawed' written in this book."

Lars said, "Over the years, my family has suffered greatly from forgetfulness and various illnesses."

"Yes, mine too. My Dad is slowly fading," replied Darius, as he took a closer look at the book.

"We are in the beginning stages of getting a team together to make the trip to that cave. We could certainly use your expertise."

"Okay," said Darius. "Who knows, this may be the missing piece."

"Great," said Lars. "I will inform the council." As he stood up, he held out his hand to Darius, and the two men shook hands to seal the deal.

Lars said to him, "Thank you, Darius."

"Just call me 'Dar'. If this helps our people, it will be all worth it." Then Lars left.

The GOL returned two days early and caught the council unawares. He discovered his mansion had been broken into, and he was truly angry. There was no one to blame but the Flawed, he said to himself. He set out to find the thieves, but nobody was talking. In his frustration, he ordered that all residents of the entire Solar Complex be tattooed with a number on the left hand in order to be able to buy food and clothing, but he would cancel the order if they gave up the names of the thieves and returned his stolen items. The council met, worried and unsure about what to do next.

In the next few days, one of the young ones had a visionary word, and the word was to leave the Solar Complex. The Flawed began preparing. The next day, the GOL found out about the plan for the Flawed to leave the Solar Complex, and he gave orders for his fully cladded soldiers to fight and to detain them, but the Flawed were ready for him. They had been preparing for this day. Men and women revealed the weapons they had been hiding in their root cellars, and a lengthy fight began. It lasted for two days, but the Flawed were determined they were not going to live in tyranny anymore. The fully cladded armoured soldiers were not as fast and nimble as the flawed for their armour had weighted them down.

The GOL was defeated, arrested, and locked up underground. What was left of his army was ordered to either leave the Solar Complex or be locked up like their leader. The defeated forces decided to leave the complex the very next day and they headed north. It was a great victory for the Flawed, and they celebrated.

But at the end of the celebrations, they still had to cope with the Darkness, and they were still called "the Flawed."

3

THE MISSION

The GOL was questioned, but he said nothing. Lars revealed to him they were the ones who had broken into his mansion and stolen the book and the keys. He told the GOL they were headed for the secret cave, and that finally got the GOL's attention. He said, in a low voice, something that could not be heard by the questioning party. "What was that?" Lars asked, but the GOL went silent again and said nothing.

Quickly, the council met and made plans for the seven-day mission. Ten men and ten women were chosen, and five young ones were added to the group, just in case they revealed a new vision. Each of them had to study the map and keys, which were securely kept by the newly appointed leader of the group, Darius the hunter, whom they called 'Dar' for short. Lars had explained the mission privately to Dar a few days earlier, so he could get him up to speed on what they had uncovered at the GOL's mansion. Lars knew Dar as a kind-hearted and wise man, who was also a builder in the Solar Complex, and one whom the people looked up to. He would make a good leader.

After the lengthy council meeting with the mission group, careful attention and study was given to the book and the location of the cave. One of the women in the party, whose name was Gwen, asked the council if Jenny could come along on the journey. She noted Jenny was well liked by the young ones, and she would be beneficial to the mission. Gwen reminded the council Jenny was the one who acted quickly to send a note about Allicin's death.

"Sure," said Lars, "that would be a good idea. Sort of like a babysitter for the young ones." With that, Gwen left the council and headed to Jenny's home.

Gwen arrived at Jenny's house, and she knocked at the door. Jenny greeted Gwen at the door and invited her inside. "Hi, Gwen. What is going on?"

Gwen replied, "I suppose you have heard of the recent events in the Solar Complex and how we broke into the GOL's mansion?"

"Yes," said Jenny, "that must have been a little scary." Jenny remembered the GOL's threatening voice.

"Yes," replied Gwen, "it was a little. But to get to the point, we have found what may be a game changer for the Solar Complex. We have a secret book and keys that we found inside the GOL's mansion."

"Okay," said Jenny, sounding a little confused.

"Well," said Gwen, "we are planning a journey of seven days through the woods, and we would like you to come with us to help with caring for the young ones. Our mission is to help the Flawed and find the cave on the map."

Jenny's eyes turned very wide, and she said, "Yes! I would love to join the mission. I can help with the young ones, and I can keep records to inform the council later. When do we leave?"

"Tomorrow morning," said Gwen.

"Okay," said Jenny, "I will be there."

The next morning, Gwen, Darius, and the rest of the party were assembling their things for the journey. Provisions, and horses, and all the essentials were getting prepared. As they were in various stages of readiness for the journey, Gwen spotted Jenny walking towards them with her horse. She had her knapsack on her shoulders with a notebook tucked in her front jacket pocket and sort of a smile of not knowing what see had signed up for.

Dar said, "Good morning, Jenny. It is great to see you."

"You too," she replied, as she reached the party. As Jenny approached the young ones, they were also excited to see her, and each of them greeted Jenny as they chattered together. Dar checked his pocket for the special keys Lars found in the GOL's home, and then placed the leather-bound book in safe keeping inside his jacket pocket. After the final goodbyes were said by the group's family members in the community, they all got ready and mounted their horses.

As they prepared to head for the seven-day journey to the cave, they anticipated a great trip with much enthusiasm and the hope they could find the solution to their predicament. The group slowly meandered through the forest floor amongst the tall trees that grew very tall, especially alongside the rippling river. Every now then, they could hear birds chirping and an odd fox or small animal running from the group deeper into the woods. Dar was in the lead, and from time to time, he would take out the map and survey the surroundings then fold it up and tuck it back into his pocket.

Dar spoke to Gwen and said, "It sure is peaceful in the woods," as he breathed a big breath of fresh air.

"Yes," she said, "I must agree with you."

After a long day of travelling, they were starting to get a little weary, and it was beginning to rain, but they were fortunate enough to find a small cave for shelter. The group took off their wet coats, and some of the men and women started a fire for warmth. The horses were unpacked and fed, then they all sat down for some supper. The glow and warmth of the fire was very welcome.

As they ate their food and were chatting among themselves, Dar noticed the glow of the fire illuminated a phrase painted in red on the small cave's wall. It read "Beware of the Elds." Dar stood up immediately and asked the men to quickly look outside. They cautiously approached the mouth of the cave very carefully but noticed nothing. A new sense of worry came over the small group, and they were cautious and committed to guarding the entrance to the cave while the rest of the party turned in for the night and slept.

Up early the next morning, the small company gathered their things and started the journey once again—but with a little more diligence than before. Dar took out the notebook with the map and got his bearings, and the group started riding once again. Along the way, one of the men managed to hunt a deer and dressed it in the woods for that night's supper. Dar followed the winding path on the map, and soon they discovered a waterfall, which they crossed over. They all filled their water bottles and had a little rest.

After the rest was over, they walked for a few more hours and said to themselves, "Will we ever get there? We are getting a little tired, and a rest would be good right about now."

"We should be looking for another cave, for shelter and a place of protection from these so-called Elds— whoever they are," exclaimed Dar. They walked a little further and were grateful to discover another cave.

"Wait," said Dar, "first we have to check this cave out." Two men from the group, with torches lit, slowly walked into the cave and returned with grim news and sad faces.

"What's the matter?" said Gwen.

The men reported, "Well, you might as well come in. It's safe in the cave, but we have new writing on this cave wall."

The group reluctantly walked into the cave entrance and shined the torch on the writing, which said, "You have crossed the sacred waterfall into our land. Leave now while you still can." The women became worried about the warning and wanted to leave with the children, but Jenny comforted the young ones and reassured them everything would be okay. Meanwhile, the men looked around the cave and went deeper inside but found nothing. They lit a fire and cooked some of the deer. While the group ate, they discussed their situation and what they would have to do.

"We need rest," the men said. "It's been a long trip, and according to the map, we are making good time. The map shows a cave by a very tall oak tree—that is where we enter and where the Secret Book of Knowledge is. We cannot turn back, no matter what."

"We are tired," the women said, "and the children need rest."

"Yes, agreed. Let's take it easy for a while." They ate

supper and settled down but always while minding the entrance of the cave for any movement.

The next day, after the much needed rest, the men of the company studied the map during their morning breakfast and said, "We need to find the opening by the big oak tree that leads to the secret cave." They finished breakfast and started the journey again, trying to make as little noise as possible in the forest.

While travelling along the path, the company spotted something coming toward them. Dar gave word to hide in the woods near the edge of the path. "It's a tall figure," Dar said, as the company was on edge. As the figure approached, it spotted the company, turned around, and headed the other way. Two men from the company gave chase, and they tried to catch the tall figure, but it ran too fast for the men. They were exhausted and gave up the chase, collected themselves and returned to the group. They said, "It was too fast for us." And after a little rest, they continued along the path.

In a short while, they spotted the opening by the big oak tree, but the entrance was overgrown with alder bushes. They managed to clear the bushes and entered the cave. They lit a torch and travelled to the end of the cave and discovered a wall with a round-arched door that had two keyholes.

Immediately, Dar pulled out the keys from the GOL's mansion and inserted them into the keyholes.

As he turned them, he heard the door unlocking. Gently, he pushed the big round-arched wooden door, and it creaked and cracked, most likely from its lack of operation over the years. When the door was fully opened, all he could see were cobwebs and a dusty table illuminated by the dim light shining through small holes in the cave, which were covered by glass. Dar swept the dust off the table, revealing it was made of marble. It was placed in the middle of the room, and it had a special, colourful prism beaming from it.

As they walked into the room, the outside door creaked and cracked as it shut behind them. The young ones under Jenny's care did not seem to notice but were drawn to the box on the marble table. As they looked and gathered around the table, they saw the inscription on the box was inlaid with brass letters that read:

"Only one key will reveal the mystery of the Flawed. It must be inserted by a young one."

Dar handed the keys to Jenny, and Jenny called to one of the young ones, named Bea. As she knelt in front of Bea, Jenny asked if she would like to open the box and remove the cover to reveal the Book of Secret Knowledge. Yes, she nodded, as Jenny guided her to the table and with the key opened the box.

Immediately, the room shone very brightly, and a gentle gust of wind blew away all the cobwebs that covered the inside of the cave. At the same time, they could hear the outside round-arched door lock shut. The windows that had been dust covered were now illuminated with a low glowing amber colour, as the group focused on the Book of Secret Knowledge.

The group carefully surveyed the book. Dar blew a little dust off the front cover, which revealed a message.

"One page per young one."

After careful inspection, Dar instructed one of the young ones, with Jenny's help, to open the first page.

The Book of Secret Knowledge

Jenny asked Bea again, "Would you like to turn the first page?" Bea nodded yes. With her small hands, Bea grasped the ancient book's cover and opened it slowly. Its edges cracked as she turned to the first page. The first page was made from pure gold leaf, and it said in bold letters:

Page 1

You have made it! You are brave! But beware of the Elds. Now the Elds know you have found the Book of Secret Knowledge which they have been looking for. They also know you hold the keys in your possession. If all things are going as planned, you should be in the glow of amber, because the glow of amber is a warning for them, like a siren's alarm. They now

know you have turned the first page, and they are
looking for you because they have been awakened and
are aware that something in the air has changed. But
do not worry, if the amber glows, you are safe.

"Great," said the men, "we have awakened the Elds."

Dar said, "If we have awakened the Elds, who or what, was that we encountered in the woods?" The men and women pondered their situation, not knowing where and when or who these Elds were. Or for that matter what would they do next. Dar said, "No matter, we must move forward." So Dar instructed Jenny to continue.

Jenny removed Bea from the table's edge and called for a young boy named Luc, another young one, to sit at the marble table for the second page opening. Jenny placed Luc at the edge of the table and guided his small hand, and he opened to the second page of the Book of Secret Knowledge. When it was fully turned, the glow of amber in the room increased slightly to a brighter glow, and it was apparent on all our faces.

Page 2

Amber is a death sentence to the Elds—they cannot
go near it. But you will need another device, and
it will be granted only if you are found worthy of
opening the rest of these pages.

Dar read the words on the page out loud so the company could all hear. On the bottom of the second page, it read in bright red letters:

Only open each page with one young one at a time. Do not be tempted to use one young one for two pages or your quest will be terminated.

Dar said to the group, "This must be important—to stress it twice." Then, he returned to the book and continued to read:

There are only seven pages in this book. Read them carefully!

Jenny had another young one ready, and her name was Alva. She was moved into position at the table, and with Jenny's help, she slowly turned the ancient book to page three. The amber glow turned the room to bright emerald green, and the click of a drawer unlocking on the front of the table caught the attention of the group. They opened it and discovered thirty small leather bags.

The men removed the small bags and opened them, and inside each bag they discovered a perfect one-inch cube of amber. As they took some of the cubes out of the bags, the faces of the women and men holding the cubes shone with the glow of amber. They took the thirty small leather sacks, distributed them evenly to each member of the party, and stored them safely.

At the bottom of the drawer, there was a green skeleton key, which Dar added to the two keys he already had. The page was glowing green, with gold letters and a bold heading that read: "How to be Unflawed."

"Finally, we are getting somewhere!" the group said excitedly. The third page had information about the key. It read:

Page 3

This green key will only open one cave in all the Solar Complex. But with much fear, I am sorry to tell you the cave, and the box inside of that cave, is in the Elds' possession, on Mount Hemor in the outer Solar Complex. You have awakened them, but the amber will help, and your young ones you will need! Good luck!

The Flawed group was a little excited, but there were still more pages to be turned. Dar said, "We are in a bad situation now—we only have five young ones with us, so we can only open two more pages." The group pondered that for a moment, and Dar said, "We have no choice, we have to open the last two pages."

Jenny was ahead of Dar and had selected another young one, named Alley, who was placed into position to open the fourth page. Jenny brought her to the table and reassured her, as Alley's hand slowly turned the page. Then the bright green, emerald light slowly turned darker and darker as the fourth page was fully opened. The cave was completely dark, and outside they could hear giant steps pounding the ground, getting closer and closer. The cave then shone bright amber, and they heard voices in an unknown tongue giving shouts of war in unison, as if preparing for battle. The Flawed were worried, and they wondered, could this be the Elds? Jenny and the other women cuddled the young ones to comfort them, and the men were silent.

The fourth page appeared almost fluorescent, and with the bright glow of amber, it looked to be three dimensional. And it read:

Page 4

By now the Elds are outside, but do not worry—your amber is your protection. If you remove the amber from the leather bag, you will feel it vibrate and it will begin to glow. This is how you know the Elds are close by.

I want you to view the Elds through the amber windows. They cannot see you, but they know something is active because the book has been found. Study them, just to know what you are up against.

Dar, Gwen, and the men and women took slight

glances at the strange-looking creatures, who were tall but not as tall and scary as the GOL. They were very foreign to them indeed. They slowly and quietly backed away from the small window, because they were a little scared they might be seen by those creatures. Dar whispered quietly, "Let's get back to the business at hand, because there is still more info on page four," as they cautiously returned to the book. Page four continued:

> Mount Hemor is the place of the Elds, and in that mountain is a cave that holds the secret of how to be unflawed. Your Flawed generation will most likely have to fight the Elds to be unflawed. You will have to gain access to the cave inside Mount Hemor and open the door of that cave with the green key, which you should have in your possession now.

The men and the women turned to each other very sadly and said, "How are we to fight these creatures—we are peaceful and ordinary family folk. How can we become men and women of war?" The cave filled with quiet discussion over the book's words.

After many conversations about the whole experience that day, Dar said, "No matter what, we agree we have to finish this journey." They sat down and ate but were very exhausted. The young ones decided to rest and sleep, and so did Jenny.

After the much needed rest, the next day was off to a good start, and the group was very eager to delve into page number five—they knew it was the last page they could open now, so they readied the last young one. Jenny called to Wren and positioned him at the table, and the bright light of amber reactivated once again. Jenny helped Wren, and he turned to page five.

There, on the opening of page five, they saw a crest with a coat of arms. It had one purple and one red sword crossed over each other, and a green key, a cube of amber, and the Book of Secret Knowledge. Once the book was fully opened, ten hidden doors in the cave suddenly appeared around the company, and a large trapdoor opened on the cave floor. Suddenly, the bright light turned to a glowing red. The message said:

Page 5

You are far from your complete resting place, for what lies ahead of you is great pain and loss, but there will be rewards. In these ten doors are ten suits of armour with ten royal purple swords. Be sure to keep the amber with the suit for complete activation of the swords—they go hand in hand when you are in battle. The ten suits must be divided equally between five men and five women. For this war against the Elds, all hands must be united. The swords will instantly vanquish an Eld, but if you lose your amber, you will have to decapitate them.

At Mount Hemor there are another three hundred
suits, along with their amber activation cubes and
swords. But, most important, you will have to bring
this Book of Secret Knowledge. Place it on the table
inside of the cave at Mount Hemor, and make sure
you have your young ones present. Do not open it
here or anywhere until you get to that cave. For your
journey, you will find under this table is a vest to
carry this book. Inside the vest pocket is a map that
shows the location of Mount Hemor.

Lastly, you have drawn the attention of the Elds,
and most assuredly, they are waiting for you outside.
Use the trapdoor in the floor, and it will bypass the
Elds through an underground tunnel. But if you
find they are at this entrance, the amber will vibrate
a warning ahead of time, so you will not be caught
unawares. The swords in your hands will guide you.
I suggest you clothe yourselves in your armour now.
Good luck!

Dar and the group slowly read the last page
again and pondered their situation. Then after much
conversation between themselves, they closed the
book and retrieved the vest from under the table.
They made sure the map was there, and they studied
it for a while. Each of the men and women put on
the suits of armour. Immediately, they felt a sense of

empowerment and, as they pulled their swords from their sheaths, they heard the tinkling of steel.

The group looked at one another and spoke with surprise, "I guess, we are soldiers now?" Dar closed the Book of Secret Knowledge and placed it in the vest, along with the map and keys. He put on the vest and wore it over his jacket. The women, with Jenny's help, got the young ones ready for the trip back home, and they exited through the trapdoor in the floor very cautiously and quietly.

4

THE LONG JOURNEY BACK HOME

DAR AND THE SMALL GROUP WERE LOADED WITH knowledge and could see they finally had a destiny, one to be revealed to the council upon their arrival, but it was still a long way home. The Flawed were careful as they walked through the tunnel, not knowing what to expect at the end of it.

As they approached the end of the tunnel, they saw light that brightened the entrance. As the men and women walked, they had their hands on the swords, but the amber was not vibrating, so they walked forward carefully. One of the soldiers decided to go ahead and check out the exit of the tunnel, and he carefully walked outside to have a look around. Upon further investigation, he found there were no signs of any Elds, or anyone, for that matter. The company arranged themselves with five soldiers at the back and five in the front, and they placed the young ones in the middle with Jenny. Organized for the journey, they continued on their way home.

They made a little distance between them and the place of the secret cave but kept moving with determination. The trees were very tall, providing shade from the sun. The canopy blocked its rays from the forest floor, which was exceptionally soft with faded moss. As the group travelled alongside a small river, the sound of the rippling water was very soothing. They could also hear the odd bird chirping.

After a long walk, they decided to take a rest and sit for a while along the side of the riverbank. One of the men was admiring his newly acquired sword, and he took the amber cube and removed it from its leather bag. He handled it, held it in his hands and was captivated by it. The amber started to vibrate and glow brightly. He immediately knew there was something wrong and almost dropped it. He managed to put it back in the bag as he shouted, scared, "We have company!" Then, his purple sword started to glow, along with all the rest of the cubes and the swords of the Flawed.

Out of the deep woods came five towering Elds. They were also holding swords. Jenny immediately gathered the young ones to her and hid themselves in the bushes, where they watched the swords of the Flawed that glowed purple.

Dar was first to reach the lead Eld, and they clanged swords together. Dar moved swiftly, and he reacted with precision and deadly force. As the Eld was defeated, it disappeared into a big puff of dust, just as the sword passed through its body. Then in turn, each of the newly minted soldiers cut into the Elds, who also immediately vanished with a puff of dust, which fell to the forest floor.

The small battle ended quickly, and victory had been won. The Flawed placed their swords in their armour suits, and they could hardly believe what had just happened. They were overcome with relief and joy and sheer terror all at the same time.

They said, "What was that?" The men and women were amazed by the strength of their armour and swords.

"I do not know," replied Dar, "but when the amber glowed, it gave me a rush of energy, and the sword just wanted to go—I followed it, it wanted to fight, and it guided me and compelled me to victory." They all agreed they had the same feeling.

The young ones, along with Jenny, came out from hiding in the bushes. Jenny was in utter amazement as she turned to the soldiers and said, "That was incredible to my eyes. You were awesome!" The group then inspected the remains of the five Elds and soon discovered what looked like five little piles of silver dust where the Elds had each been defeated. They gathered up the dust and agreed it needed to be examined by the council when they reached home.

"We better get moving, just in case the Elds we killed managed somehow to get word back to their base."

Within a short journey, the small party arrived at the outer edge of the Solar Complex where the lookout tower was situated. The guards noticed them and blew the loud trumpets to let the village know they were back. The company passed through the gate and into the safety of the village.

"We made it!" they said, as their wives, and husbands, and the other young ones came out and greeted them. The group separated and went to their respective homes for a much needed rest.

It was not very long before the council leader, Lars, was knocking on the door of Dar's house.

He said, "I heard the trumpets and came as soon as I heard." Overcome with excitement, Lars said, "Well, did you find it?"

Dar replied, "Boy, did we ever."

"How was it?" Lar asked impatiently.

"Before we get into that, we have been gone a while—did anything happen while we were away?"

"Sad to say, we lost one of our own. She was at the archives studying, we received a note at the council explaining what happened, of course we have to keep her identity a secret, but she is dead.

"That's terrible news," said Dar, "Who was it?"

"It was Allicin," said Lars sadly.

Dar put his head down and said, "She was a nice lady." After another moment, Dar finally spoke again, "There is so much to explain." He walked to his vest and pulled out the five bags of silver dust. He gave them to Lars and said, "I want you to get this examined, to see what exactly it is."

"Okay," agreed Lars, "but you do have good news, right?" Lars was smiling again hopefully.

"Yes," said Dar, "I have really good news and really bad news."

"Explain, please," said Lars, now looking worried.

"Well," said Dar, "We encountered an alien race, but we do not know how many there are. And to stop the madness in the Solar Complex, we have to fight these beings, to gain access to their mountain, where there is another cave." Dar continued, "There is so much to explain—I am very tired, as we all are. We have things to tell that cannot be rushed, and we need rest."

"Yes, I understand you. Then please take your rest," said Lars, and he hugged Dar excitingly and said, "I knew you could do it, my friend. But tomorrow we want a full report."

"Yes," said Dar, as he showed Lars to his front door, and Lars turned around and said to Dar once again, "I knew you would come through for us!" as a big smile came across his face.

Dar patted Lars on the back and said, "Maybe you will go on the next trip," and they laughed as Dar closed the door.

A knock came on Dar's door early the next morning. Sure enough, it was Lars. He had two cups of coffee ready, and Dar opened the door and said, "I guess you want to come in."

"Yes," he said, "here you go," as he handed Dar the coffee. They sat down for a moment as he was getting prepared for the council meeting. "What's this?" said Lars, as he looked at the suit of armour and the vest with the Book of Secret Knowledge lying on the table.

"That, my friend, is the key to our freedom and to putting an end to this madness. Come on," Dar said, "we will be late for the meeting, and I am sure everyone will be there."

"Yes, you bet." said Lars. Dar gathered up the suit of armour, along with the sword and vest, and the map to Mount Hemor.

They both walked into the front entrance of the village hall where the council had gathered. Dar walked up to the front of the room and placed the items on the table in front of him. Lars stood up first and began to speak. "I do not have to tell you why we had to go on this expedition—ever since we raided the GOL's mansion and discovered the ancient book and the keys there was no doubt this character has been responsible for, or in some way connected to, our years of being downtrodden. Dar and the members of the group that risked their lives to bring us some important news have returned and have some great news, and some not-so-great news." Then, the audience went noticeably quiet.

"Please," said Dar, as he stood up to the podium, "We started this journey not knowing what to expect, but we continued and travelled seven days into the wild. We were tired and managed to find a cave and, as we lit a fire, we saw a warning—beware of the Elds—we had no idea who they were. Now, before I go any further, we found the cave we were looking for and, in that cave, we found this book."

As Dar took it out of the vest and held it up the audience was encouraged, and Dar went on to explain the book contained seven special pages that could only be opened by seven young ones. "We only had five young ones to open the pages, but we have pages six and seven left to reveal the mystery as to why we have been kept down all these generations and why we are not doing so well. But the remaining pages have to be opened in another cave deep within the Elds' territory." A slight gasp was heard from the members of the audience.

Dar said, "Please bear with me. While we were at

the cave, as we turned each page, this book revealed some instruments we need to fight these Elds. On the table before you is a suit of armour, and inside that suit is a small amber cube." Dar reached in the pocket and took out the amber and showed it to the audience.

Then he said, "This cube will glow when one of the Elds appears or is close by." Dar held up the sword and said, "This sword will glow purple and, along with the vest, turns an ordinary man or woman into an expert soldier. We have experienced this firsthand and have defeated five of the Elds." The audience clapped and was very encouraged.

Dar turned to Lars and asked him, "Did you have the silver dust examined?"

"Yes, I did last night, right after I left you. And— after examination—it is pure silver, but the funny thing is, it's the same quality of silver we mined here in the Solar Complex a long time ago."

Dar said to the audience, "Do you have any questions?"

One member said, "What's next?"

Then he said "In short, we must take the Book of Secret Knowledge to Mount Hemor, along with the two keys and this green key, which opens the cave at Mount Hemor. We need two more young ones to open the remaining pages, six and seven, but—and I say 'but—we will have to fight the Elds. We have no choice but to put together a small army of men and women and try as best we can to defeat this curse."

Alban piped up and said, "We have been making swords for a long time now, because we knew this day would come."

Dar said, "The only swords that will kill an Eld are the ten swords we have."

"That's not enough," said another member, sounding worried.

"Yes, we know," said Dar, "but, we have been assured by the book that three hundred more suits are waiting in Mount Hemor."

"This sounds like a trap," said Alban.

Dar said, "Well, just how much more of this madness can we take? At least now we have hope—we have a map and swords, plus this suit, which I can attest turned me into a warrior. That is all I have. We have accomplished a great deal, but a better day awaits us just a little further ahead."

Dar sat down and his friend, Lars, stood at the podium and thanked the members of the expedition, and Lars said "We have to convene and discuss our next plan. Agreed?"

And all the council said together, "Agreed."

The next day, Dar was called to the council again, along with the members of the original group, for a private meeting. The council had come up with an idea and wanted to see what the group thought of it.

As they sat down, Lars said "First of all, you have had a tremendously successful journey into the Solar Complex. I have been in awe of the items you have managed to bring back. We have been giving this some thought, and we feel a spy mission to the proximity of Mount Hemor would make the best use of our talent and time. We figure ten of our best people would be able to bring back a full report of how many of these Elds you speak of and just exactly where they are situated. They will be under secure cover, with complete stealth."

He turned to Dar and asked, "What do you think? That would buy us some time and help us here to recruit some very capable men and women."

Alban the council member said, "We have been training some recruits, and we would like you to come and see their progress. We have made some exceptionally good swords, and our blacksmith has been working non-stop since we got the news of the GOL's mansion. Before we adjourn the meeting, are we in agreement about the secret mission?"

Dar thought for a moment and said, "It would be good to know what we are up against. Yes," he said, "that would be okay. But I want to see these hand-crafted swords." He looked at the other members of the group, as if to say, this should be good, then they left the meeting hall.

Gwen said, "I am heading over to the training camp to see these recruits and the blacksmith's new swords."

"Yes, good idea," said Dar, "I will be there shortly. I have to go home first, and I will meet you there in a moment."

The group arrived at the training facility and watched the young men and women spar with each other. The craftsmanship of the swords was very good. The blacksmith was there, taking pride in his creation and describing the material and the heat of the flame that went into making it.

By and by, Dar showed up with a box and placed it down by his feet as he watched the sparring continue. The sparring then stopped for a minute as the recruits got a much needed drink of water. Dar stepped into the sparring court and talked with the recruits. He asked them how swords felt.

They said, "It's light and very strong." Dar looked at the blacksmith and gave him a nod of affirmation.

One of the recruits asked Dar, "How was the expedition?"

"Funny you should ask," he said, "for, when we were away, we received some items I wanted to show you." Dar proceeded to the box, and he brought it over to the sparring court. He opened it up and there were two suits of armour, amber cubes, and the two swords.

"Wow," said the recruits.

"This is the game-changer." He held up the sword.

"Can I handle it?" said one of the recruits.

"Yes, sure," said Dar, and handed it to her. Then the blacksmith, out of pure curiosity, came over and asked if he could see the sword.

Dar handed it to him, and the blacksmith said, "Purple metal!"

"Yes," said Dar, "and in battle—in the presence of an Eld—it glows."

"My word," said the blacksmith, "I have never seen purple metal, and it's not of this world," as he handed it back.

Dar gave it to the recruit, and she pretended to fight the imaginary opponent and said, "I do not see any difference from the sword the blacksmith made."

Dar laughed, "You will," then he said to the recruit, "Here, try on this suit of armour," but he never told her about the amber.

She buckled on the suit of armour and immediately felt empowered. "Wow," she said, "what is this feeling?"

"That's good," said Dar, "you have activated it."

"Activated what?"

Dar said, "We do not know. It is a complete mystery to us, but this suit works and empowers us."

"How?" she said.

"Here, let me spar with you," replied Dar. Dar took the blacksmith's sword, and they went through the motions. The swords clinked and clanged against each other, but the young woman recruit was in total control.

In wonderment at the new armour, she said, "It's like this suit knows what to do by itself—it's amazing and effortless." Dar reached into the suit's amour pocket and pulled out the amber.

"Wow," she said, "what's that?"

"This is the key. Listen very carefully," Dar spoke to all the recruits standing around him, "this cube is your protection against these enemies called the Elds."

"Who are the Elds?"

"We will get into that later, but for now you have to have this in your suit at all times. When you fight these Elds with the amber, they cannot win. But if you lose this cube, you will have to decapitate them. One more thing—this cube will vibrate and glow when it senses the presence of an Eld."

"That's amazing," said the recruits.

"Yes," said Dar, "I will reveal more to you over the next few days. I will be giving a public talk about the expedition and what lies before us. Do not worry, we will let you know fully about our plan." Dar told each of the recruits to practice with the two suits and get familiar with them, then he left.

Dar secured his armour at home and headed for the jailhouse where the GOL was being held. He was granted access to the lower level, where he wanted a meeting with the GOL. The GOL was escorted by armed guards to a small room, he was handcuffed, and chained to the floor.

Dar said to him, "We finally got your pals, the Elds, on the run, and your whole system is about to crumble." The GOL did not speak but just looked at Dar. Dar said to him, "We know you killed one of ours in the archives."

The GOL replied, "Dead people leave no clues."

"I figured you had your hand in this. That is all I wanted to know. You will be charged for that, and you will never leave here." Dar turned away and left.

After Dar left the detention center, he headed for the council chamber and, upon arriving through the doors, he received word his father was in the hospital and not doing so well. He headed for the hospital as fast as he could. When he entered his father's room, he could see that he was doing badly. Dar took a chair and started to speak to him. His father barely recognized his son.

"Dad!" he said, "It's me, Darius. You were doing fine a short time ago. What happened?" His father did not say much. Dar's sister appeared in the doorway and spoke to him.

She said, "Just before you went on the expedition, and after the GOL disappeared for that short amount of time, that's when Dad went downhill fast. Many people we knew have lost their memory, and his memory disappeared too. He hardly knows me, and I have been looking after him for a long time."

"I know," said Dar, "you have been exceptionally good to him and me, but I think I know who is
responsible for all of this." He held onto his father's
hand and was deep in thought.

The next day, Dar's father took a turn for the worse,
and Dar took it awfully hard. The council under-
stood, and the speech he had to give to the village
was put on hold. In the process of dealing with his
father being unwell, Dar had a little time to put things
together in his mind. As he waited by his father's
bedside, he thought of the expedition and the silver
dust, the increased deaths amongst the village, the
whole scenario.

After much reflection, Dar got up early and suited
up in full battle armour with sword and amber and
headed for the detention center just one more time.
He summoned the guards with authority and said,
"Take me to the GOL."

They went to the lower level, where the GOL was
still locked up, and as Dar made his way through the
doorway, the GOL spotted him in battle armour and
screamed, "Where did you get that sword and suit?"
Then, Dar pulled out the vest that held the Book of
Secret Knowledge. The GOL could not contain himself and shook the bars of the jail cell and went into a
fit of anger. While the GOL was in his fit of rage, Dar

pulled up a chair and sat down. The GOL eventually calmed down, finally exhausted from being angry.

Dar spoke, "Are you finished? Just sit down, you idiot, and listen to me for a while." Dar pulled out the glowing sword and pointed it at the GOL, and he said, "This sword is quite remarkable. I had no idea of its power until I fought and killed five Elds." The GOL went into a frenzy again, but Dar just sat back in his chair, much amused.

He pulled out the amber, and it was glowing. "Hmmm," said Dar, "that's interesting. This only glows when Elds are present, so I guess you are partly an Eld. Do you want to know what is funny? When I killed those Elds, there remained a small pile of silver dust. I had it examined, and it's silver alright, but they also told me it's the same silver used to be mined here a few years back. Any comments on that?" The GOL said nothing.

"Last but not least," Dar said, "I have something to show you," as he reached into his vest pocket and took out the map to Mount Hemor, and that set the GOL off again. Dar waited a moment to speak, "My father is not doing so well, and now you are going to pay for that. We know where everything is, and we are going for it. Whatever you did when you went away, we are going to reverse and get to the bottom of this. We, the Flawed as you call us, are on the rise." And with that, Dar got up and left.

The GOL said in a shrill scream, "You will pay for this with your life."

"Bring it on," Dar said, as he closed the jail's lower doors with a tremendous slam.

The next day, Dar headed to his friend and council member, Lars, and sat down for a while. He asked the council member if he could have permission to draw up a set of plans to make a battle shield, with the two purple swords, the Book of Secret Knowledge, the amber, and the green key for the upcoming war with the Elds.

"Yes," said Lars, "that's a good idea. I will check with the council for funding. In the meantime, go see the blacksmith and get his thoughts on it."

Then the council member said to Dar, "How have you been since your dad has taken sick?"

He said, "Not too good. I know what causes his trouble, and who is responsible, that is what drives me. Now we have got to fix this Solar Complex, because this has gone on far too long. There is no future living this way. It has been a long while since we heard anything from the young ones—the last vision said they see someone coming—I wish they would hurry up! But now we have a little hope with what we have discovered, and we must act on it. If this vision the young ones had is accurate then we can hope for something there also, but in the meantime, set up the podium and get the day ready for the event. We need recruits, and they must volunteer to fight our way out of this. It's time, don't you think?"

"Yes," said Lars, "I will get on it."

Soon after, Lars gave a press release about the recent expedition to the outer edge of the Solar Complex. He said, "Dar will be giving a speech on what he found there and the challenges that face all of us." The news of his speech spread like wildfire, and on the night of the great meeting, all were in attendance.

Dar was ready to deliver his speech and, after the council member announced him, he walked up to the podium. He cleared his throat and thanked the council for the opportunity to present his findings on the recent expedition and thanked the audience for coming to hear him.

He began to speak and said, "As you all know, we have had some difficult times here in the Solar Complex, and recent events have made things a lot worse. First, I would like to put your mind at ease and to let you know we have arrested the GOL." He paused while everybody cheered. "I believe, with all my heart, he is the cause of all our troubles. I do not know how he is doing it, but we are going to find out. On our recent expedition, we raided the GOL's home and found evidence of another place that holds the keys to our troubles—the forgetfulness, the mental confusion." And the crowd overwhelmingly agreed.

"Our first expedition was a success, and we did find a great treasure of information, which revealed we have to go on a greater expedition to fully know how we can be unflawed—if that is at all possible."

"So, why am I here?" exclaimed Dar. "I cannot do this without you. We need one hundred and fifty men and one hundred and fifty women to volunteer for the next step of this journey. We will also need a reserve membership of one thousand recruits. I will not fool you; it will be hard, and some will die, but we must fight for our future and our way of life, such as it is now. In short, we will have to fight an enemy to gain access to an unknown treasure we hope is there—we do not know for sure, but we must find out. So please help us, and in helping us you will be helping yourselves.

"That is all I can say about the expedition for now, but all the three hundred recruits and the one thousand in reserve will be fully briefed. So, I am asking you to sign up at the local council and be ready for training to begin immediately." When Dar finished his speech, volunteers rushed to the council to sign up, and at the end of the day, they had filled their quota.

5

THE SPY MISSION

WITHIN A FEW DAYS, THE TEN-MEMBER SPY TEAM was ready for the secret mission to see how many Elds were at and around the area of Mount Hemor. They had met with Dar, and he gave them as much advice and information as possible. The spies were also given a copy of the original map. They were fully capable and eager, and they set off. The team left the Solar Complex under the cover of night and disappeared into the woods.

In the meantime, the recruits, all three hundred and the one thousand in reserve, were at training camp to learn how to swing the purple swords and fight. Dar was there with the full suit of armour and said, "You know, it's counter-intuitive, because the suit of armour does most of the work. The real reason we are training you is for you to get rid of the nervous energy, because I know none of you have ever been in a war, and this will be a war for survival, and the future of this the Solar Complex, and your family, your neighbours, and life as we know it."

Most of the recruits stopped what they were doing and gathered around Dar to hear him speak. He said, "For the first time, we have something to go on, we have a little hope and that is what we never had before. I look around at you, and most of you are not married, but someday you will be. I want you to think about your parents, grandparents, and all your relatives, because I know they have all been affected by what the GOL has done to us and them over the years. We have a chance to correct this curse—and that is what it is—a curse."

"So, train, and prepare yourselves like the rest of your life depends on this. And, when it all comes down to it, it does depend on what we do here today and when we go to war. We must take the mountain, for in that mountain is a cave, and the first five pages of the Book of Secret Knowledge tell of another three hundred suits with swords and amber to help us fight against the Elds."

"We must also bring our young ones to open the Book of Secret Knowledge, because we must find out what is on the remaining sixth and seventh pages. We do not know, and it can only be opened by them. So now you know why we must go and find out what has been causing all this trouble in our lives for genera-tions. I can see how this curse has affected everyone, including myself, but I am determined to see this to the very end. So, fight, I say, and train to the best of your ability, as best as you know how." Dar's speech was finished, and the recruits thanked him for the encouragement and the information.

As training continued, day in and day out, the recruits learned about the amber cubes and the swords, along with the suits of armour. Dar dropped by to show the recruits the shield the blacksmith had created.

"Wow!" They said, "that looks very good."

"Yes," said Dar, "the blacksmith outdid himself." The shield was a shiny silver with two purple swords in an X pattern, the Book of Secret Knowledge was on the top, between the swords, and the amber cube was on the right-hand side, and the green key was on the left. Then Dar said, "Each recruit will have a shield for added protection."

As Dar was showing off the shield, word came along with the trumpet call from the outpost of the Solar Complex that one of the spies had returned. Dar left immediately and hurried to see him.

When he got there, the spy was in bad shape and resting on a bed. "What happened?" said Dar.

The spy said, "We were travelling as stealthily as possible, but we were ambushed, we never had a chance. I managed to get away, and I hid undercover for two days until I felt safe enough to move."

Dar sat down and thought for a moment, and said,

"We will have to move up our timeline." He told the spy to go home and get some rest, and then Dar left and headed for the council.

The next day, during the training sessions at the edge of the town, Dar asked the recruits who were wearing the suits if they were getting used to the feeling of empowerment. "Yes," they said.

During their training routine, out of the corner of his eye, Dar spied some Elds off to his right in the woods, and then he spied some on his left. Suddenly, they decided to close in and attack the recruits. The Elds jumped the high fence and started towards them, swinging swords and yelling war cries, but the recruits who were wearing the suits of armour had been forewarned by the vibrating amber and responded instantly to the Elds' aggression. It was over in a matter of minutes. Dar could only watch with his mouth open wide, because he had never had a second to warn them.

After it was over, he said, "That was amazing!" He ran to where the fight had just happened, and the recruits were in awe.

The recruits who had the suits on said to Dar, "The suits just took off, and we knew exactly what to do—it was precision and speed—it's like the suits have a genuine hatred for these creatures."

"You just got a crash course in what these suits can

do, and, in some way, I am glad these Elds showed up, and now, I bet your confidence has grown." Dar then said to the recruits, "Come with me for a minute, I want to show you something else." They followed him to where the Elds fell, and on the ground was the silver dust—there were ten piles of it.

The recruits looked and said, "What is that?"

Dar gathered up the dust and said, "This is pure silver. I have to get this to the council." But before he left, he said to the group, "Be on the watch, there may be more Elds. They know we have the book, so be on the lookout!" Dar carefully spied the woods once again. "Looks like they may be bringing the fight to us."

Dar returned from the council with haste, and with all the suits and swords. He picked out five women and five men and said to them, "Wear these suits at all times, sleep with them, if you must. We have to guard all four corners of this complex, because I know they will come again." The recruits chatted amongst themselves about what happened, and they talked about it all night. How the suits performed, and how, with precision and swiftness, it reacted with their bodies.

Dar gathered the council members for an emergency meeting and said, "We have to get moving on this trip to Mount Hemor. The Elds are coming closer, we do not know if this was a rogue attempt by some misled Elds or if it was planned. We have sent the recruits with the suits to the four corners of the complex, but the spy mission was a total failure without the suits. I figured they would be okay going stealthily, but it did not work. So, our mission has to include six suits on the recruits and the other four to stay and watch the corners of the complex."

"Yes," said the council, "let us get moving on this right away."

The volunteers had been contacted—one hundred and fifty men and one hundred and fifty women, from all walks of life. They were instructed to prepare for a journey through the wilderness—they did not know the outcome or if they would even be successful. Many of them had never seen a time when they had to fight, because they were a peaceful community, minding their own business. But times had changed, and they knew it.

As one of the volunteers said in the preparations, "Desperate times calls for desperate measures," for he knew what was required and, for that matter, they all knew what was required. They had been preparing for over two weeks, but some felt they were not ready and were a little nervous going from living a quiet life to life as an all-out soldier, preparing to fight a war. They had been talking this over now for a little while. To the older generations, it seemed that was all they talked about—always the same talk—of how it used to be.

The young men and women with thoughts of fighting were starting to feel it. Sometimes you could cut the tension with a sword and, now they had a date, they were resigned to the fact that they were going to war. The young ones came with their mothers and fathers, and they were missing each other already. They knew something was different, and the parents tried to explain to the young ones why their dads and moms were leaving—they tried but the young ones did not understand. The horses were fed, and the saddles were filled with provisions for the trip.

The small army of volunteers saw Dar coming towards them with his horse in tow. He met them and asked if all was going according to plan.

"Yes," was the scattered shout from the group.

"Great," he said, "because we have been waiting for this day for a long time, and we leave tomorrow morning for Mount Hemor. I take it you have studied all that we have gone over, the map, the swords and our mission in general?"

"Yes, we are certainly ready for that aspect. You have taught us well."

"Okay, get a good night's sleep. We are off in the morning."

Dar quickly headed to Gwen's home and knocked

on her door. Gwen opened it and asked Dar to come in. She asked him, "What can I do for you?"

Dar replied, "We need Jenny again. Do you think she would come with us to Mount Hemor to mind the young ones?"

"I will ask her," said Gwen.

"Well, we are leaving tomorrow morning. I know it is a little early, but the recent spy mission was a failure, and we must act on this right away."

"Okay," said Gwen, "I will go to her after supper."

"Thanks," said Dar, and then he left.

6

The Journey to Mount Hemor

MORNING CAME FAST FOR SOME, AS A LOT OF THEM were not prepared to leave, and there were some tears and sad goodbyes, but the whole village came out for the departure. They decided on ten young ones, just to be sure they had enough. Dar arrived with the vest and the book, along with the three keys. Three suit bearers were at the front of the party, and three others were at the back, including Gwen and Jenny, while the rest of the suits minded the four corners of the complex, in case of a surprise attack from the Elds.

Dar was ready and spoke to the village and his army of three hundred volunteers in a short talk. "We know what we have to do. We are as ready as we can be. We have a great chance to change history here. Please, pray for us as we leave and hope for our safe return." The villagers waved and shouted farewells, as the volunteers saddled up and rode out of the village and disappeared into the woods.

The first day of the journey was clear, as they travelled through the thick forest in single file through the small path by the meandering, rippling river. The trees were very tall, and everywhere they looked the greenish-brown leaves blocked out the sun's rays. The carpet of brown moss where the horses' hoofs treaded was soft and quiet. The group was very sombre, for they knew not what awaited them around the next turn. As they travelled, some of the group members engaged in small talk, but Dar soon made it clear he wanted it to be quiet while they listened for unusual sounds.

At the end of the day, they camped by the river and after much thought, they decided to light a fire to cook supper. Dar figured the smoke or bright lights might attract attention, but the group was getting hungry, so they blocked the fire as much as they could with a wall of rocks. Some men tried to catch some fish in the nearby river, but they had no luck. The mood lightened up a bit as Dar reassured them with his wit and stories from his past around the campfire, and that helped them turn from nervousness to confidence. The young ones were playing together as the women tried to get them ready for bed. Dar gathered some of the party around the fire, and he took out the map and went over it while the fire provided the light for instructions. Shortly after, he set up the night watchmen with the suits for the first night's stay away from home, in the deep woods of the Solar Complex.

The next morning, they relit the fire, while Jenny and the other women were getting the young ones ready to start another day. The rest of the group was in various stages of waking up and stretching. Some were washing up by the edge of the river, and some men were in the water bathing themselves. The horses were tended to, and a quick check was made by roll call, and all were accounted for. Breakfast was prepared, and all were fed. Clean-up was fast as they got ready to start another day's journey to Mount Hemor.

The slow walk through the woods was suddenly interrupted as a flying arrow came out of nowhere and stuck in the trunk of a tree, by the edge of the trail. That caught Dar's eye, so he halted the quiet march and rode his horse to the arrow. He got off his horse and looked around very carefully to see if there were any more arrows coming. He walked to the tree and took off the message attached to the end of the arrow. He opened the rolled-up message, which read: "To the Flawed horsemen, go no further. Danger awaits you." He folded the message and stuck it in his pocket.

"What did it say?" asked Gwen.

Dar said, "They are scared because they know we

are coming! We are not turning back, so let us get to it." And they mounted their horses and started the journey again.

The group rode for another half-day and came to a nice place by the river, with lots of room and plenty of wood for a fire. They set up camp, and Dar went for a visit to see Jenny and the women, to reassure them not to worry. While there, he spoke to the young ones in a calm, reassuring voice, like that of a father.

Nighttime came quickly, and soon all were asleep. The fire still had embers smouldering away, which produced a light smoke that went high in the sky through the canopy. Frogs were groaning, and crickets were chirping. Then a sudden cry from one of the young ones caught the attention of Dar, who ran out of his tent and towards the child.

"What is it?" he said. As he spoke outside the tent, a woman opened the tent door and stepped outside to speak to Dar. "Does she have a message or vision?" he asked.

"Yes," the child said, "at the forks of the river below."

Dar repeated, "At the forks of the river below." He thought about that for a while and said, "Is that it?"

"Yes," she said, and the child went back to sleep.

"But, that's good," he said, "It's something." Dar slowly walked over to the fire for some light and took out the map and surveyed it. There he found the river that divides into a fork. Then he said to himself, "At the forks of the river below. What does it mean?" He spoke it over again and again. He finally got tired and went back to his tent.

The next morning, Dar had a cup of coffee while pondering the child's message and sharing it with other members of the group, but nobody had any answers for that riddle. They once again mounted up and started the ride. Dar was in front, and as they were making progress, he saw the fork in the river, just about a quarter mile in front of him. As they advanced, the area closed more tightly, as the mountains squeezed the path closer together.

Dar noticed the trees. It looked like many of them had been cut. He thought of the young one's vision. "At the forks of the river below." Then, he said in a frantic voice, "Everybody off their horses! Now!" As they were dismounting, giant logs came towards them in a swinging motion from out of the forest and just missed the men and women as they fully dismounted, but none were hurt.

When the logs finally came to rest from the pendulum swinging motion, Dar said, "At the forks of the river, be *low*." It makes sense now." He walked to the swinging log, almost still now, and stood underneath it with his hands in the air, then pointed to the logs, saying excitedly, "Be low, *under* the logs." All the logs, ten in total, came to a complete rest, and the group resumed their travel. Dar said, "We owe our lives to that young one."

They passed the forks in the river, and off in the distance, they could hear thunder as the clouds began to darken. Dar spoke to the others, "We will have to find shelter and fast. Weather is coming." They turned the bend in the river's edge, and as luck would have it, they could see a giant cave. With that, a sense of relief came over Dar, and he said, "Let's head for that cave, and get in there and start a fire. It will be cold shortly."

They made time and secured the horses as they came to the cave and prepared for the storm. The lightning had started, and the wind picked up as the rain poured from the sky. Some of the men found old trees and started a few fires. Dar said, "We need more wood," and with the help of the other men, they ventured further into the cave as the lightning lit up the cave in flashes.

Suddenly, the amber glowed and started to vibrate, the swords turned a glowing purple, and someone shouted, "Elds!" Immediately, a host of Elds came from the tunnels from all directions into the cave as the lightning flashed and illuminated the Elds' angry faces. As they came, they were screaming blood-curdling sounds. Dar removed his glowing purple sword from its sheath and flew into action. Elds were dropping like flies as the suits did their bidding.

The rest of the recruits each had their own battles

against the enemies going on, all at the same time. They could hear the Elds vanishing, and the silver was illuminated by the lightning flashes as the dust dropped to the cave floor. More Elds rushed the Flawed from other tunnels as the thunder roared, but the recruits were ready and met the challenge.

It was over in a matter of what seemed to be minutes. All the Elds were dead, and Dar held his sword at the ready and asked everyone to stop and listen. Then each of the Flawed, with swords at the ready, stopped and listened. The only thing they could hear was the steady pouring of rain and thunder crashes, along with the bright lightning illuminating the cave walls. The lightning revealed the silver dust in piles all over the cave's floor, and the armoured women stood with Jenny, once again holding the children closely in a guarded corner of the cave.

A few moments later, Dar deemed it safe, only after the amber stopped glowing and the swords returned to their normal colour. "We are clear." he said, as the men and women soldiers placed their swords back into their sheaves. The lightning was still flashing when Dar gave the order to rest for a while, and then he appointed men and women to set up a night watch.

When the morning came, it was sunny and bright. The Flawed were getting ready to leave but not before they collected their spoils of war. They gathered the seventy-five piles of silver dust that lay on the cave floor. All the silver was divided evenly amongst the group, so it wouldn't be too heavy for one of them to carry. Under Jenny's direction, the women attended to the young ones, just to see if they were okay after the terror that had occurred last night, but they all seemed to be okay.

Dar had a glance at Mount Hemor, which could be seen in the distance. "It's about another day's journey, and then we should arrive." Before they left, he spoke to them in the cave and said, "We are getting close to that mountain, I would expect them to be more numerous than before, but who knows, I guess we'll proceed as planned." The horses had been fed and were ready to move again. The party mounted them, and they were on their way.

As they followed the river, Dar unfolded the map and checked out the surrounding landmarks as they corresponded with the map. He then folded it away and returned it to his vest. As they travelled, Dar noticed strange markings on the trees and carvings into rocks that were not mentioned on the map. He found it rather strange and wondered what they meant. The other members of the group made remarks about the signs. They continued, but they felt a light vibration in the amber, and Dar said, "Does anybody else feel the amber?"

"Yes," they said. Dar took out a monocular and

spied ahead, and he could make out, in the distance, three figures on horseback.

"Quickly," he said, "Let us hide in the trees and the surrounding bushes. But we will continue with just a small party to see what they are about." Dar dismounted and waited for the three figures to arrive. The closer they got, the more the amber glowed. He had an idea and said to the rest who were with him, "We cannot let them know we have the book and swords." So, he hid the vest and the book in the bushes, along with the swords, but they were kept close by just in case they needed them.

The three figures arrived and, sure enough, they were Elds, but they were not surprised at the group's presence. They stopped and looked at Dar, and Dar looked back at the Elds. Then one of the Elds spoke, "Are you the Flawed?"

The small group with Dar answered, "Yes."

The Elds said, "Why are you so far away from your home?"

Dar spoke up and said, "We are off to the outer limits of the Solar Complex, looking for plants and herbs to create medicine for our community, which has developed a sickness we cannot cure with the plants and herbs we currently grow."

"I can assure you; you will not find any here."

"Well," said Dar, "do we have your permission to make our way through your land to find such plants?"

The Elds said, "I think you need to turn around and head back to where you came from."

Dar said, "We have come too far to turn back now. How about we give you some monetary substance, and you can forget we were ever here?"

"What do you have in mind?" said one of the Elds. Then, Dar held up one of his fingers to motion for the Elds to just wait a minute.

"I have something for you." He then reached into his pocket and said to one of the Elds, "Here, catch this." And he threw the small bag of silver into the air that contained two dead Elds worth of dust.

The Eld managed to catch the bag and opened it and said, "Looks like the silver I have in my pocket already." Dar was very curious and said to the Eld, "You have silver like that?"

"Yes," said the Eld, "we all have silver."

Dar had to ask the next question—it was paramount. "How did you get this silver, if you do not mind me asking?" The Eld paused for a moment and he looked at the other Elds. Dar and the other few men that were with him were ready but unsure what was going to happen next.

The Eld finally said, "We are all miners from another land, and we have been here for a long time."

Dar said, "How did you all come to be here?"

The Eld said, "We were promised a fortune in silver, and we were hired to mine it."

"Who hired you?" replied Dar.

"We do not know his name, but he is not from around here. Nobody knows where he came from," then the Eld sort of laughed and said, "Ha, a long time ago, he fooled you Flawed and took over your mineral rights to the whole Solar Complex, and then he hired us to mine it." He laughed again at the small party and said, "That old geezer double-crossed both of our peoples, but we managed to steal some of it, and we carry the silver in our possession wherever we go." Then the Eld's demeanour changed, and he said, "No, we do not need your silver." The Eld started to sound a little angry, and his voice became louder. "We have our own silver, so you are not permitted to pass into our land!"

After that comment, Dar figured he had all the information they would give. But now they would not let him pass. Dar spoke gently as he could and said to the Elds, "We need to get moving so we can find the herbs and medicine for our people." The Eld spoke even more harshly towards Dar. He motioned with his hand and said to them, "You leave me no choice," and he ran towards them. At the same time, he picked up his sword hidden in the grass, and the other soldiers followed suit as they picked up their swords which immediately started to glow purple. The Flawed fought the three Elds in a close battle but defeated them without suffering any injuries. At the end of the fight, Dar asked the soldiers to gather the silver dust that remained on the trail, along with the bag he had thrown to the Eld.

"We could not let them return from where they came—they could have blown our cover, and we have to keep very low," explained Dar.

The others said, "Our suits were burning on us—they wanted to fight."

"Yes," said Dar, "I held it off as long as I could while I was pumping them for information. I was surprised they gave it to us so freely. So, that GOL hired these Elds to mine our silver, then he double-crossed them, and us. What a great guy! His mother must be so proud," laughed Dar. "There has to be a record of this somewhere. I had no idea about this." said Dar. Then all the others from the group came out from the bushes and the woods, resuming their travel together once more.

Continuing along the path by the river, the Flawed edged closer and closer to Mount Hemor. The group saw more images carved in the rocks. They had no idea what the images meant, but they pressed on for a little while longer. Soon, they saw the mountain clearly through the cover of the trees. There was a large open field between them and the mountain. Dar spread the word to lighten off the horses and rest while they surveyed the surroundings. Then he took out his monocular spyglass and looked at the mountain, up and down.

He could see the cave, and the big wooden door to the entrance. He also saw Elds guarding it on both sides. There were more Elds on the ground level of the mountain, coming and going. He retracted the monocular and sat down for a moment and said, "This is going to be very hard."

One of the soldiers asked to borrow the scope and viewed the situation, "I see what you mean," he said and gave the scope back to Dar. "What's the plan?" he asked the leader.

"Well, one thing is for sure—we are not marching out into that open field. I guess we'll wait until dark and try to move in a little bit closer for a better look."

"Good idea," the Flawed agreed and waited for sunset.

While they were waiting, one of the recruits had an idea and approached Dar and asked, "Why don't we dress up as Elds and openly walk into the mountain and see what we can discover?"

Dar thought it over and asked, "How will we get an Eld uniform or clothes? They vanish when we strike them, leaving nothing but silver."

"I have an idea," said the soldier. "If we leave our amber with you, we take the risk of not knowing if we are in the presence of one of them, like you taught us. But, without the amber, we'll have to take off their heads, therefore leaving the clothes for the taking."

Dar thought for a moment. "Man, I do not know,

but it could work. It's worth a try. I cannot think of anything else." He looked at the recruits and asked, "Who will volunteer for this mission?" Three recruits said they would go, and they handed over their amber. Dar said, "I will only let two go. We need the amber for the soldiers, because we do not have very many." Dar handed one of the soldiers back his amber cube.

So, the two volunteers got ready under the cover of nighttime and headed out very quietly to look for a few unsuspecting Elds. The recruits followed the edge of the field, keeping their eyes wide open for any movement. Luckily, it was a full moon, and the forest was not totally dark. The recruits heard the chatter of some Elds and crept upon the conversation.

Just behind them, in the brush, there were five Elds. The soldiers looked at their swords, and they were not glowing. The suits were not activated, but the recruits waited, and waited, and eventually three of the Elds left, and the other two sat down for a rest. Then the two recruits surprised the Elds, coming through the bushes brandishing their swords, they easily decapitated the Elds. They just fell to the ground but didn't disappear, and the recruits recovered their uniforms.

The recruits returned to the main group with the prize. Dar was the first to greet them and said in a whisper, "Well done," and he handed them back their amber. Dar studied the Elds' uniforms and said, "I think this will work." He tried on the whole uniform. It was a little tight as it went on over his armoured suit.

"It works," he said and asked for another volunteer. The original soldier who first had the idea insisted he join the scout mission. The two men got ready in the Elds' uniforms, and they also had to cover the purple swords so when they glowed, they would not be seen. But they had to take the amber for protection, just in case. The helmets were also a little tight, but they fit.

The two then left the cover of the forest, and Dar said, "Let's see if we can fool anyone who is keeping watch." Both walked through the edge of the forest and walked down the large field without any trouble. "So far, so good," said Dar. When they reached the edge of the mountain, they blended with the Elds, but kept a safe distance so as not to draw attention. They ventured out, away from the main cave and found another path that led to the back of the mountain.

It took a little extra time, but they did eventually make it back to the main group. The recruits were on guard and almost had an altercation with the scouting party, but Dar took off his helmet to show he was not an Eld and revealed his face and spoke to them. When he got the Elds' suit off, he quietly spoke to the rest of the group and said the best way to get in was around the back of the mountain. "There were not very many Elds there."

Then one recruit spoke up and said, "If there are

not very many Elds there, why don't we bring five of our young ones along with five of us soldiers? Two of us can wear the Elds' uniforms, and we can act as prisoners for a surprise attack. Then we'll get to the cave and hand out the rest of the three hundred suits."

Dar said to the recruit, "You are brilliant! That just might work. Okay, let us get this planned down to the last detail and then initiate."

Daylight came early for the group on the edge of the field as they made the plans for that night's quiet attempt to breach the cave at Mount Hemor. The Book of Secret Knowledge was revealed, and the three keys and the plan was set up to go around the back as prisoners of the two Flawed dressed up as Elds.

"We will go first, and then you follow close behind, watching our progress just in case something goes wrong and the Elds discover us. Then we'll be in an all-out war to take the cave. We all go tonight, when the Elds are sleeping and there are not many on guard. When we get the other suits, put them on immediately and be ready." Dar said, "Are we all clear?"

"Yes," they said as the two got ready in the Elds' uniforms.

Dar had another recruit wear the Elds' uniform as he installed the vest that held the Book of Secret Knowledge and the three keys. Jenny and the five young ones were prepared, and the five soldiers and the two dressed up as Elds stood ready.

They began travelling the back route to the cave, along with the rest of the party a stone's throw behind. They made their way around the mountain very cautiously but steadily, as the two dressed up as Elds led the way. As they walked, they saw two Elds appear from out of the woods, from another path that they hadn't noticed.. The Elds approached the prisoner party and questioned the two Flawed dressed up as Elds, then they quickly moved aside to let the group pass. Dar drew his sword from the center, behind them, and vanquished the two unsuspecting Elds.

They continued, and after a while, were approaching the entrance of the cave where they saw four Elds standing guard. Dar said to the others, "You two walk up slowly, and the two of us will walk behind you. When we get close, we will appear from behind and strike them down."

So in the middle of the night, with all of the recruits close behind the prisoner party, the two recruits dressed up as Elds walked towards the cave's entrance and the four Elds standing guard there. The guards said something the recruits could not understand, but they continued walking towards the cave. When they got close enough to the Elds, the purple swords began to light up the night. Then Dar and the other recruits came out from behind the two Flawed dressed up as Elds, and they vanquished the four, quick as a wink.

Dar sent one recruit to go and get the others, as he

pulled out the green key from his vest and approached the big wooden door to the cave. Dar heard the steps of the recruits as they came close to the cave. He said, "You recruits with the armour, protect this entrance with all you have until we get to the other suits. I do not know how long that will be." And he motioned the young ones to go with Jenny and soldier women.

7

Fighting for Freedom

DAR THEN INSERTED THE GREEN KEY INTO THE
wooden door and turned the knob. It opened with a
creak and a crack, like old wooden doors that have not
been opened for a long time. As he entered the cave,
he pulled the keys from the keyhole, and he heard a
low voice speak. The creak of the old door shutting
behind them sounded like the word, "Welcome!" At
the same time, the cavern was illuminated, and Dar
saw the sacred table in the centre. Then he proceeded
into the room.

As he quickly placed the keys in his vest pocket
and retrieved the Book of Secret Knowledge from the
back of his vest, he placed it on the table. The book
locked into position, and the table glowed aqua blue.
Dar then asked Jenny to prepare the first young one,

whose name was Marley. In a calm voice, Jenny asked Marley to come right away, and she sat her down at the table and guided her hands to turn to the sixth page. Dar was getting a little stressed as the sweat ran down his face, not knowing when all hell would break loose. The young one turned the sixth page fully open, revealing the words:

Page 6

*To the Flawed, a great and terrible curse has been
placed upon you by the Giver of Lies and the Elds.
Together, they have had access to alien technology and
have weaponized this mountain against you for most
of your generations. The Giver of Lies and certain
members of the elite Elds have discovered how to
create a low frequency that affects the mind of your
kind. That is what keeps you Flawed; you have never
known about this until now—it has been kept hidden.
But the secret is here. All you must do is turn it OFF,
and that is on the last page, seven, but you will have
to use the youngest of your young ones. That is, if
you have brought enough of them.*

Dar could not believe his eyes as he scanned the door to the cave entrance and asked if everything was still quiet. Then, he silently received the A-OK, and he quickly asked the women, "Who is the youngest young one?" They enquired and gathered a young boy named Julian to come forward. Jenny brought him to the table, and he began to open the book to page seven.

Then they heard a loud cry outside the cave's entrance, and a recruit said, "I can see Elds! Coming! They are coming by the hundreds!" As the amber glowed, the swords turned a glowing purple once again. They were engaging the Elds at the entrance of the cave. Dar could hear the silver flying as the Elds dropped one by one. In the meantime, the others were fighting and trying to gain some time for Dar. He then looked at the young one, who was a little scared of all the commotion and had not yet turned the page fully open.

Dar rushed to the child and asked Jenny to help him to please turn to page seven and open it fully. With trembling hands, Julian turned it and, when it was fully open, a big stone dropped out of the cave wall and onto the cave floor, and another door was revealed.

Dar rushed to the door and quickly opened it as the whole cave was glowing bright amber, and with the excitement of the moment, the hair stood up on the back of Dar's neck. He looked into the room with amazement, and he could not believe his eyes. "Suits!" he said. "Armoured suits!"

He called loudly to the other recruits, "Get in here, we found the other suits." They came rushing in as Dar handed the armour out, complete with amber and purple swords. As the recruits put them on and immediately joined in the fight, the Elds came in from all directions. The Flawed recruits came as fast as they could, and soon all three hundred suits were actively fighting outside the cave. As the silver dust flew everywhere, all Dar could hear were swords clanging and tingling against warring, angry Elds.

Dar was frantic and nervous and said out loud, "What now? What's next?" He had forgotten about reading page seven and said, "How can I be so stupid? Concentrate," he said to himself and rushed to the book and started to read. In the amber-glowing room, he read,

Page 7
Get the suits for the rest of your party.

"Done." He said out loud to himself, and he read further to see what the book instructed him to do next.

Open the door at the end of the suits' secret chamber.

He rushed into the secret room that had held the three hundred suits and looked around. Sure enough, at the end of the cave, there was another door with three locks. "Oh, great!" Dar said, and he searched for his keys frantically. He quickly ran forwards to the other door, inserted all three of his keys, and opened it. Once the door was opened, he heard a humming sound coming from the entrance. Dar tried to enter the door, but he was held back by a force field of some kind. "Oh, can it get any worse?" he said, and he rushed back to the book and started reading again.

You cannot enter the last door unless you disable the force field. You disable the force field by placing the first finger of the young one who turned page seven in the middle of page seven.

Dar looked at Julian and took the child's first finger and placed it in the middle of page seven. He ran back to the last door at the end cave, and he entered it. The cave then glowed bright white, then there was another table with another dust-covered book waiting ahead of him. He went inside and gently blew the dust off the book, which revealed the words on the front cover: "How to be Unflawed." Dar could not believe it. He wiped the sweat from his brow and said, "We made it!" He was out of breath.

"Now what?" As he looked around, he did not know what to do next. He was still looking around the cave but found nothing, only the book. "I cannot touch it," he said to himself. "Young ones," he thought to himself and rushed out the door to the other Book of Secret Knowledge. He thought of the fighting and worried he was running out of time.

As he reached the other book, one of the women

said to him, "That page seven you were looking at turned into another page when you left through that doorway."

"Wow," Dar said, "I was stumped back there, and I did not know what to do." He sat and scanned the last page, and it had a new page seven. "How can that be?" he said, as he started to read in a panicked state.

INSTRUCTIONS

You have made it! You are in the glow of amber, and the fighting outside is great. I hope you have prepared and discovered all that you need up to this point. The force field must be down to uncover the secret book in the other cave, which leads to another door containing the last book. I take it by now you have discovered this already.

I know your nature and how nervous and reckless you become when you are frantic and scared. As you go through the final door, where the last book is, victory is not too far away, but you must have three young ones and a soldier with amber and a purple sword. A young one, once again, must open the book to page one—the only page you need to read.

So, Dar selected the three remaining young ones who had been waiting with Jenny. As the fighting continued outside, they hurried and made their way to the last cave where the last book waited. They entered the bright room, and it turned amber and four spots appeared on the floor at all four corners of the table. A phrase was projected on the cave wall that read:

Three young ones on the spots,
The soldier takes the red,
The young one on his left,
Then the page is read.

"A riddle," said Dar. "Great!" He wiped his brow again as he stepped on the red spot. Frantically, he said, "We are so close." He thought about it for a minute as he tried to gain his composure, then Dar turned to the young one to his left and calmly said, "Can you please open the book to page one." She reached out her hand and turned the book to page one, then a sliding door appeared on the wall, along with the last instructions, which read:

This mountain, at one point in the universe, was a
meteor that landed here on this planet many years
ago. It is radioactive and has been weaponized. There
is no other metal in the known universe that has the
capability of such force. It has been triggered and
manipulated to give off a low frequency that bothers
the minds of the Flawed.
In dangerous hands, this can be an awfully strong
weapon, and they found it and used it against you. It

causes forgetfulness and early symptoms of memory
loss. The lever you now see holds the key to your lives
and your future generations. Simply turn the lever
from the Flawed position in the opposite direction
to the Elds, which will reverse the curse onto them.
Note, all four of you around the table must turn this
lever at the same time.

Dar gathered the three young ones and himself and turned the lever away from the Flawed to the opposite position. Dar then released the lever and breathed a deep sigh of relief. He got up and walked out of the room, completely exhausted, and sat down.

Jenny said to him, "Now what?"

In a matter of minutes, the recruits came running into the cave and said, "All of a sudden, the Elds started holding both sides of their heads and dropped their weapons and ran into the woods. And at the same time, I felt a great relief come to my mind and body. What was that?"

Dar thought to himself, "I felt the same thing as soon as I turned that lever in the opposite direction."

Then the rest of the group came running in and asked, "What just happened? We were fighting the good fight and suddenly, the Elds held their heads and just ran away. What happened?"

Dar said, "Come with me, I want to show you something." As they made their way back to the last cave where the lever was switched, they were amazed and relieved. They all had their turn in visiting the cave that held the lever. Dar said, "We have to guard this with all our lives. I expect by now living in the Solar Complex has taken on a whole new meaning. I wish I were there." Dar was very anxious to step outside of the cave, and as he started to walk out into the glow of amber, then to the bright sunshine, all he could see and feel as he walked on the ground was six inches of pure silver. It felt like walking on a sandy beach. He looked out over the wide field. It was also covered with silver.

He walked back into the cave, and it never really sunk in—what they had just accomplished. Dar said, in wonderment, "We did it! We reversed the curse—it is on the Elds now. It's our turn now." Dar sat down and finally rested from the arduous task.

After a small discussion with Jenny and a few soldiers, he got up and headed to the table and placed the Book of Secret Knowledge in the vest. When he took it off the table, all the glowing amber lights went out, and he removed the three keys as he headed for the outside and placed them in his pocket. He spoke to the soldiers outside and said, "We are safe for the first time in our lives. The tide, I believe, has turned in our favour. I have never been in this situation before." As he spoke to the recruits and the young ones, they were all in an incredibly happy mood, which he noticed, and that had never happened before. Dar did not know what to do next. "This is very new," he said, "I guess we rest and head out in the morning. Let us get all the fine details worked out first. I want one hundred—no! One hundred and fifty armoured soldiers to guard this cave." Dar sent out a few scouts to check out the perimeter to see if there were any attempts by the Elds to take back the mountain.

Then there was the silver issue, "What are we going to do with all that silver?" He thought for a moment and ordered all the soldiers to gather the silver and store it in the nearby caves but place into their possession as much as they could carry back to the village, and he asked for the soldiers to guard the entrance of the cave. One final look around, and it was time to prepare to head home.

8

WE ARE GOING HOME

THE NEXT MORNING, ALL HANDS WERE HELPING each other get ready for the long-awaited trip home. They were extremely excited, and the mood was rather cheerful. Jenny and the young ones were playing as the soldiers gathered all the provisions and readied the horses. Dar went to the cave and filled his satchel bag with ten pounds of silver dust to show the council the spoils of the war. As they bade farewell to the one hundred and fifty soldiers who would remain to guard the caves, they set off for the victory ride home.

While riding through the forest, Dar noticed right away that new growth had started to appear, and the sky was turning bluer, and the grass was turning greener, and the rivers were not so dark as they used to be, and all the dead brown leaves had fallen off the trees and new shoots had appeared. But one thing was especially clear. There was nothing in the air—no low frequency. Dar's mind was clear, and his thought process perfect. He breathed the very fresh air and shouted out into the forest, "Victory at last!"

And all the group repeated "Victory at last!"

When they finally arrived at the outpost of the Solar Complex, they found it was deserted and the guardhouse gates had been removed. They looked in amazement, there was nothing but silence. Dar said, "Let's get to the village." And the soldiers rode as fast as they could.

When they arrived the village was in total carnage. The village had been burnt, and one could hardly recognize it. They dismounted the horses and were in a frantic search for survivors. Dar headed towards his father's house, and there was nobody home. He remembered the root cellar out back and went there immediately to open it. There he was greeted by his father, who looked rather worn and tattered, but he said, "My boy, you made it home!"

Dar said, "Dad! You recognize me!"

"Yes, why wouldn't I? You are my son."

Dar hugged his father and asked, "Where is Mom?"

"They took her," he said, "and most of the village."

"Where?"

"Who knows? I tried to get her, and they overpowered me, but I managed to escape in just enough time to get to the cellar."

"Who overpowered you?"

"They call themselves the Elds. They wanted to know how you got the Book of Secret Knowledge and the keys, especially the green key. They questioned everybody."

"What about the armoured soldiers?"

"Well, they were at the four corners of the complex," said Dar's father. "Which is far away from us. We were simply ambushed."

"Where are the soldiers?"

"They are a worried bunch of souls and feel defeated for letting the village down. They never knew anything about the attack. They are over in the old jailhouse. And, by the way, that GOL character—they busted him out of the lower cell."

Dar thanked his father and asked him, "Dad, how do you feel?"

"Well, son," he said, "it was the other day, I felt my mind just come back to me. I remembered everything, and I started to feel good. I got up out of the hospital bed and walked home, and started to do some gardening, and the next day those Elds showed up. So here we are. What are you going to do?" asked his father.

"First, we need to find the remaining people, if there are any. And, Dad..."

"Yes, son?"

"We are no longer called the Flawed, that's over."

Dar went outside and met the others who were coming out of hiding. He reassured them as best he could and gathered them to sit and talk about what happened. They were all frightened and scared but relieved to see Dar. They said, "It happened fast. During a nighttime raid, they dragged us from our homes. Most of us, as you can see, managed to hide. They kept on asking us, 'Where did you get the Book of Secret Knowledge and the keys?' Nobody said very much, but they took many for ransom and said, 'if you want to see your loved ones again, we want the book and the keys, but most of all we want the mountain.' It was sort of painful for them—they kept on holding their heads as if something bothered them."

"That's my next question to you—how do you feel?"

"Funny you should ask that. A day before the raid, we all felt like a great weight had been lifted off our minds."

"Yes," said Dar, "we turned off the frequency that bothered us for generations, and the pain the Elds now feel, that's what we used to feel." Dar said, "We are no longer called the Flawed, but the Freed. A new normal has begun for us, and we have total victory over the Elds, but it looks like we have some unfinished business." Dar asked the remaining survivors to help look for other survivors, if there were any. Then he got up and headed for the old jailhouse.

As he opened the door, he found a group of defeated men and women who felt like failures. Their heads were down in shame as Dar opened the door. Then he went in and sat down by the soldiers and spoke. "I wish you could have been there in that cave. How we defeated the Elds and how we turned off that mountain—it was incredible, to say the least. I guess you felt it?"

"Yes," said one of the soldiers, and remarked at how good it felt, "and my memory came back to me."

And the others said, "Yes, mine too."

Dar said, "I do not blame you, because how was I to know what the enemy would do? We had a limited number of resources and only ten suits. Do you know how many suits we have now?"

"How many?" one recruit asked.

Dar replied, "We have three hundred and ten now."

"Wow." they spoke. "The mountain has been incredibly good to us, now that we have switched it over to affect the Elds. We found out about the silver and where it came from. And the death toll from the Elds, well, let us just say the caves are full of silver, stacked up to the roof."

The recruited soldiers were starting to feel a little better. Dar reassured them and said, "Don't worry, you will get your revenge on these Elds, because we are going after our family, and this time there will be no surprises."

That night, over a small village campfire, Dar and the victorious soldiers explained how they defeated the

Elds and took Mount Hemor, with its secret caves and the Book of Secret Knowledge, which Dar had in his possession and showed to all. The villagers had plenty of questions, and Dar answered them all. The young ones played with the three keys, and the teenagers were enamoured with the purple swords, as they practiced play-fighting with each other. After a great night of conversations and talking to the people who, for the first time, had no ill effects that the darkness caused, life in the village had the beginnings of the new normal.

Up early the next day, Dar set out for the council. As he was walking, he noticed an older gentleman walking towards him. Dar knew right away who it was and said, "Abner, what are you up to?"

"Dar, so good to see you," he said and was all smiles as he walked up to him and handed Dar four nice sized trout.

"What's this?" asked Dar.

"Fish," said Abner. "I have been fishing. For some reason, last week I woke up in my mind, and everything was good. I walked outside and said out loud, 'This is what I remember!' Then I grabbed my fishing pole and walked the mossy path along the river. I cast my line and, you know what? The fish are back!" Then Abner looked around and said, "Where is my house?"

"While you were fishing, the Elds destroyed the village."

"Ah, no worries," said Abner, "I was sleeping in the woods anyway for the past week. I feel so good, I am going fishing again tomorrow, and the next day, and maybe the day after that. See you, Dar," said Abner, "I have to go and dig some worms."

"See you," said Dar, and Abner whistled to himself as he left.

The next morning, Dar was determined to get the Elds and bring them to justice. The meeting was held in what used to be the village square. He said, "We have many suits now, and the advantage is for us, as long as the mountain frequency is against the Elds. This is what we are going to do: We'll split up evenly and head in eight different directions of the compass from this village, check every cave and turn over every rock, so to speak. I want those Elds, but mostly the GOL. They have a three-day head start on us. But we must fight this battle with full strength. We cannot risk being outnumbered. As good as the suits are, we cannot fail."

"When a group discovers where the Elds are, you will have to provide two runners in each troop, running in opposite directions, and the next group will provide two more runners in opposite directions to speed up the process, to carry the news so we are all at the same place at the same time. We cannot light fires for smoke signals or red flags on top of trees—we will be discovered. The runners go at dusk before it gets dark. It will be a 360-degree run, but we all fight in unison. It may take a few extra days, but we must be strong."

The next morning the recruits were eager and had become seasoned experts as they took on the new challenge of finding the Elds who had kidnapped most of the villagers. They headed in eight different directions at the same time and made good progress. The horses galloped when they came to wide open fields and gently rode as they ventured through the forest. The riding continued for four straight days, and at the end of each day, they waited to see if there would be any runners coming with some good news of a location.

At the end of the sixth day, in the evening, just before dark, a runner was seen coming through the woods and reached the next party with the word the Elds had been spotted on the south border of the Solar Complex. With that info, two more runners started and spread the news to the next troop, and, at the end of five days of travelling, they finally met at the south position.

They met in the forest very quietly that night and made plans for a five o'clock raid in the morning, while the Elds were sleeping. As they prepared to walk into the Elds' camp, the amber started to glow and the suits came alive, along with the glowing swords. The Elds were surprised, to say the least, and many started to fight. In the process, they were reduced to silver dust, but the rest of them knew they were no match for the members of the Freed, and they surrendered and laid down their swords.

Dar gave commands, and the soldiers gathered the Elds and forced them to sit in a circle as he questioned them. The first question Dar asked was, "Where are our people?" The Elds pointed to a large corral, and Dar rushed there and released them. They were relieved to see him, and Dar's mother ran through the crowd and hugged him.

After securing the villagers, Dar went to the Elds' elite and asked, "Just what do you think you are doing?" The Elds said nothing, but when Dar applied pressure—and a few pointed threats—one of the elite Elds, who was dressed in a different uniform, stepped up and spoke.

He said to Dar, "We had no choice. We serve the GOL. He has promised us riches far beyond what we ever could imagine, but we were deceived. As you can see, he is not here but has escaped with two others like himself, and we do not know where he has gone. One thing is certain—he is not happy you have found the Book of Secret Knowledge and the keys. He knows now the tide has turned against him, and he just disappeared—"

"Wait a minute," Dar interrupted the Eld, "the Giver of Lies met with others like himself?"

"Yes, they came, and he walked through the forest, and we saw what looked like a bright light, and when we went to check it out, all we saw was some burning spots on the grass."

"Where did he go?"

"I bet he went back where he came from," said the elite Eld.

The very next day, the Freed gathered up the remaining Elds and tied them up. The remaining villagers were fed, and they started the journey home on the soldiers' horses. When they reached the village, after five days of walking and riding, they were very tired. But no rest awaited them, for they had no homes to live in. They had to reside in the woods, with makeshift shanties of tree limbs and other natural fibres as they reunited and tried to rebuild the village.

The Elds were locked up and chained to the bars of the jail cells underground for further sentencing. The council reconvened, and the group sat down and figured out what to do next. Dar said, "One thing is certain, what we need to do right away is get our houses rebuilt, and our community back on track. We need to hire carpenters immediately and get the word out about what happened to our burnt-out town. We have more than enough money to pay for the reconstruction with the silver at Mount Hemor."

"That gives me another idea," continued Dar, as he got up from his chair and spoke to the council. "Permit me to leave for about a half an hour—I have to show you something." Dar rounded up a few recruits and headed for the jail. On the way there, he picked up a knapsack, entered the jailhouse, and went to the lower level where the Elds were locked up.

Dar said to the Elds, "We are rebuilding our town, and seeing that you destroyed it, it's only fair you help pay for it." The Elds looked puzzled and did not understand how that was going to happen.

They asked, "What do you want with us?"

Dar threw the knapsack between the bars and said to all the Elds, "Empty all of the silver you have in your possession into that knapsack." The Elds refused, but Dar said, "Does the color purple mean anything to you?" Then, with hesitation, the Elds, one by one, passed the knapsack around. From several pockets on each Eld, the silver filled the knapsack, and it was so full it hardly fit between the jail cell bars. Dar left and headed back to the council, and there he handed the knapsack full of silver to them, saying, "That should attract some carpenters and labourers."

Dar went home, and after a good night's rest, he

met with the council again and delivered a full report to them. "We are free," he said.

"Yes, we all feel it," said Lars, "but as long as that GOL is on the loose, we just do not know what to expect next." After much banter back and forth, Dar and the soldiers were thanked very much for a job well done.

Dar said, "We do not know what the GOL is going to do next. I want to see if the young ones have had a new vision or a word, because we need direction."

"Yes," said the council. "See to it tomorrow."

The next day, Dar was not feeling too good. After a bad night of sleeping in the woods, he was a little bit upset. He never got much rest, because the mosquitoes and other flies buzzed him all night. As he made his way to the young ones, he noticed just how much damage the GOL and the Elds had done to the village. As he looked around, he thought for a moment and remembered the mansion the GOL left behind. When he arrived to look at the young ones, they were not doing particularly good either, for they had received no rest.

Dar enquired whether there had been any new words or visions from the young ones. The women caretakers said, "In these conditions, this makeshift home of tree limbs is not very good, and the children are tired."

Dar thought for a moment and said, "I want you to

gather all the young ones, and make sure some of the women soldiers come with you, because we are headed for the GOL's mansion. We are going to take this for ourselves, since he destroyed our village. At least then, for the time being, you will get some well-deserved rest. It is a little journey, but it will be worth it until we get our village rebuilt. The council is in the process of getting the word out that we need help, and we have money to hire carpenters."

"That sounds like a good idea," they replied. Dar talked it over with the council, and they all agreed to go and take over the mansion, and they recommended it be guarded by twenty-five soldiers. They acted immediately and gathered what little they had and started to ride to the mansion, and as they rode there was no sign of an Eld for the two days' journey.

When they finally reached the mansion, the women were most impressed with the home the GOL had lived in. They opened the front door and made their way in and looked around. They noticed it had running water and a fully stocked pantry. The women then started to prepare food for everyone. After lunch, they looked around the mansion and discovered it had twenty-five bedrooms on the main floor and twenty-five rooms on the lower floor.

Dar said to himself, "I am moving in here and making this the base of our operation while we figure out where that GOL is and what he is up to." The women and the young ones were happy to finally have a place to stay and get caught up on their much needed rest. Dar was encouraged for the young ones and had hopes that sometime soon they would be given more visions.

After a few days of relaxation, Dar and a small group of soldiers decided to visit the village. Upon arrival, there were many in the small village asking questions about the houses that needed to be built. Dar set up a meeting with the village council and terms were met for building, and materials were to be delivered so the work could get underway. The carpenters built makeshift houses first, as a place to stay while construction was underway. As the work began, more and more tradesmen entered the village with hopes of going to work.

Dar met with the council and said, "We have some silver on hand, but we need to get to Mount Hemor and collect some more of the silver from there for the wages of the workmen. They will want to be paid shortly." He asked a couple of the carpenters to build a cart with wheels to bring the silver. Dar appointed twenty armoured soldiers, and he told them, "Take the cart when it is ready and go and get some of the silver from Mount Hemor, and while you are there, find out how the soldiers are doing and give them a report of how things are going here. Do not mention the town has been burned, but rather say we are building new homes everywhere." Within a few days, the cart was ready, and the soldiers prepared for the long journey.

The next day, there were strangers in the village, and more came every day to visit. Dar was a little curious and stopped one of the visitors and asked him where they came from. "We are from the outer rim of the Solar Complex." he said.

"What brings you to our village?"

He said, "We have been making a living, or should I say trying to make a living, farming. My parents have been sick up until last week, when everything changed."

"Go on," said Dar.

"Well, my father was a farmer all of his life, but in the past three months he got worse and forgot who my mother and I were. He could hardly form a decent sentence when speaking, but last week everything changed. I got up early, and I was going to start breakfast. When I entered the kitchen, my father was already there, making me breakfast and talking to me like nothing ever happened. After that, I went outside, and I noticed the grass was greener, and the sky was bluer. Our stream near our farm was once darkened, but the water was clear again. I was speechless. So, we decided to make a trip here just to see what is going on. Because something is different, but we like it."

Dar sat the farmer's son down and explained everything. Soon others arrived and decided to make their homes in the village. The progress was going very well, and the village was getting built. The women had spent over a month at the mansion but were now leaving because their new homes were built, and they were getting established once again. It had been noticeably quiet the past few months, and living in the new Solar Complex was a lot better than it used to be.

Life seemed to be getting back to normal when, one day, Dar was asked to come to the home of one of the women who had a young child. He entered the home and sat down, and the woman said, "All I hear her say is 'deception, deception.'"

"That's good to know," said Dar, "maybe something is about to happen. Please keep me posted."

9

Shooting Stars

After a busy day attending to the daily affairs of the village and trying to get its residents settled into the new normal, and after hearing about the 'deception' vision, Dar returned to his temporary home in the mansion, since his new house was not built yet. After eating supper, he walked out on the back balcony and admired the scenery. He sat down and rested for a while, and sleep came to him slowly. He awoke a little while later, only to see the glowing sunset as it faded, and just before dark he noticed some shooting stars here and there. But amongst the stars, he saw some objects which were not shooting stars but black objects, zooming in the same direction. Dar started to count, ten, fifteen, and then it was too dark to spot any more. This was genuinely concerning, and he made a note of what he had seen and wrote it down on paper and dated it. He was tired. He headed to bed and placed the note beside the night table.

After a good night's sleep, he woke up early the next morning and noticed the note. He read it and then jumped out of bed and readied himself as fast as he could. He headed towards the village with the note stuck in his pocket. He rode straight to Lar's newly built house, beat on his door, and waited for a reply.

When Lars opened the door, Dar walked in and said, "Did you happen to see the sunset last night?"

"No," was the reply.

"Too bad," said Dar.

"Why?" asked Lars.

"Well, I have seen some shooting stars—"

"That's nice," said Lars.

"Yes, but I have also seen about fifteen other black objects heading westward," continued Dar.

Hearing this, Lars started to pay attention to what Dar was saying. "What do you make of that?"

"I do not know," said Dar, "but one thing's for sure—it's been very quiet around here since we took over."

"You should relax," said Lars.

"I am trying to, but there is a bigger picture we cannot see."

"And what's that?" replied Lars.

"The GOL is up to something, I know it. I visited

a young one last night, and all she's hearing is the word 'deception' in her vision."

"I would not worry about the GOL," said Lars, "you ruined him well. Your house is almost ready, then you can leave that mansion."

"Yes, I cannot wait," said Dar.

"What are we going to do with that mansion? It's only an eyesore and a constant reminder of the trouble he caused us for a long time."

Dar said, "When my home is ready in the village, I say we blow the place up!"

Lars just laughed and said, "We could certainly use the land."

"You get permission from the council, and I will blow that place sky high."

"I will do that," said Lars, and then Dar left.

That night, Dar was very anxious to see the sunset and maybe a few more dark objects. This time he invited some of the soldiers for a social gathering at the mansion but said nothing about the objects.

About the same time as the previous night, as the soldiers were admiring the setting of the sun, one of the soldiers said, "What is that? And that? There's another one there, look! Right there!" He pointed at the dark objects heading west at an extremely fast speed.

Dar said, "I saw that last night, and there were about fifteen of them. Then the sun went down, and it got too dark for me to see. That's why I invited you here tonight, just to back up what I had seen."

"What now?" said the soldiers.

"I do not know, but I feel we have to let the council know we have seen strange objects, and we need to be as prepared as we can."

"For what?" they asked.

"I do not know, maybe another war!" said Dar.

Later, Dar met with the council and invited the soldiers who had seen the objects as well as all the rest of the soldiers. They sent out an alert to say, "Prepare for anything, but do not spread this in the village. Have your suits ready at a moment's notice."

With that being said, the back door of the council opened and in walked another soldier who approached the council and said, "We just got back from Mount Hemor, and we have the cart full of silver."

"Great," said the council, "we can pay the workers." And, just before he left, he said that he and the other soldiers witnessed some strange objects in the sky last night at sunset.

"Yes, we know," said the council.

The soldier said, "One of our soldiers saw it and made a sketch of the object." He took it out of his pocket and handed it to Dar.

Dar unfolded the sketch and said, "Yes, that's

it." Dar asked the soldier how things were going at the cave.

"We are holding the mountain, and it's very quiet."

"Good," said Dar, "go and get some rest." Then he said, "I wonder if I showed this sketch to the Elds in prison, would they know what it is?"

"It's worth a try," said the council.

"Well, let's go and see it right away, then." Dar got up, along with some of the council members, and headed for the jailhouse.

When they arrived, Dar approached the bars of the cell, took out the sketch, and held it up. The Elds looked at it as if they had seen a ghost, and all at the same time, they gasped.

"Aliens, of the worst kind," said the senior Eld, "and a lot more evil than the GOL. We have had dealings with this type before, and they are not good at all. They show no mercy, and worst of all, they enjoy inflicting pain."

The senior Eld continued, "I guess he is finished with us! So much for the wealth he promised."

Dar asked, "How do we fight these?" The Elds had nothing to say. They did not know. Disappointed, the council and the soldiers left.

Back at the council, the meeting resumed, and Dar said, "We will shortly know what is to become of this!"

"Why?" said Lars,

"They will tell us, but until then, we need to get

ready as best as we know how. I will be moving from the mansion and into my new home here in the village," said Dar. "Can I suggest something?"

"Yes," said Alban.

Dar said, "I have searched that mansion while I have lived there, every nook and cranny, but I have found nothing. But that does not mean there is nothing to be found. The GOL may have something there to help him get the victory over us."

"What do you want to do?" asked the council.

"I want to blow it up, so it's no use to him or anyone like him. Maybe those aliens have something there we do not know about."

"Okay," said the council collectively, "do it as fast as you can."

Dar said, "I will do it tomorrow. I have to get the charges and the wire, and we will blow it to pieces"

All the soldiers were united on a new determined mission. They worked all night and into the morning, and when the sun had risen, the whole mansion was wired with enough explosives to send it to the moon. When everyone was out of the mansion, and the all-clear signal was given, the soldiers rolled the two wires that were attached to the TNT and walked to a safe location, a great distance from the mansion.

The wires were then connected to the charger box, and the countdown began: 10, 9, 8, 7, 6, 5, 4, 3, 2, 1... BOOM! The whole house completely disappeared in the explosion. After the dust settled, Dar and the soldiers went to inspect the remains. And there, in the middle where the house used to stand, was a big hole leading to an underground tunnel.

Dar could not believe his eyes. He said, "I knew something was here all along." The company all went into the tunnel and discovered silver and storages of food. Dar thought as he walked the caves and tunnels, "There must be millions of dollars' worth of material here." They tried to find another exit, but, after exhausting every avenue, it appeared the tunnel only had one exit.

"Now," said Dar, "we have to guard this place." The next day they started to build another smaller home to conceal the hidden underground tunnels and the spoils from prying eyes. A giant fence with a large perimeter was also installed, and they turned it into a training ground for the soldiers, so the place would be always guarded. Some of the money went to pay the carpenters and the tradespeople for the mass undertaking of rebuilding the village.

A progress report was given to the council, with regards to the demolished mansion and the new training grounds.

The council also had news. "We have our new convention building erected and ready to go. We have talked about this in the chamber and have decided to honour you, Dar, along with the soldiers, for the gallantry and braveness you have undertaken for us. When you returned from Mount Hemor with complete victory, we were in shambles and could not celebrate. We were barely surviving and just hanging on, but that is over now, and we are back on track. Word has it, now that we are up and running, the whole Solar Complex and surrounding areas have felt the impact of the mountain being turned off. Our forests have returned, and the water is once again pure. You must be acknowledged for your bravery. Medals are to be given out and honours to be applied." Hearing this, Dar and the soldiers were grateful.

"When is this going to take place?"

"A week from today," said the council. "It has been set up already, without you knowing. It was a surprise. Given the recent appearance of the alien objects, we were a little hesitant but decided to go ahead with it. There is going to be a big celebration. We need something positive after all the frustration and upsets in the past little while, not to mention the generations of pain. You have earned it. We are no longer the Flawed, but the Freed."

The next day, victory banners went up all over the village, which was now fast becoming a small town. Improvements over the past six months had made an incredible difference. The council received letters from people in different parts of the whole Solar Complex, saying they were coming with gifts and tokens of appreciation for what the soldiers had done.

Dar was still a little concerned about the flying objects and continued to check the night sky. The soldiers were encouraged not to let their guard down because of the coming ceremonies and to be vigilant. The week quickly passed, and the village was full of people celebrating and thanking the soldiers, who had been treated like royalty for what they had done. The convention center was full to overflowing, and Dar and the council all sat on the stage. It was pomp and prestige to the max. Then the mayor of the village stepped up to the podium to speak.

"Men and women, councillors and soldiers, and all who have come today from far and wide in our great Solar Complex. Thank you for coming here today, it's been a long time coming." Then everyone clapped their hands. "We come here today for bravery, and to honour bravery, and to think about what we have gone through for generations. The forgetfulness, the mental sicknesses that have plagued us for generations, they are now all gone. Our forests have returned, the grass is green, and the sky is bluer than it has ever been. Our lakes are starting to see the fish that were once thought gone forever, and overall, life has improved greatly because of what our soldiers have done. On a personal note, my parents, who long ago lost their memories of me, my wife, and children, have miraculously recovered fully, and now they are enjoying their grandchildren."

Then the mayor turned to Dar and said, "This man led a charge to the mountain, not knowing if he would be successful. He and his soldiers had a large uphill battle, but they overcame all odds against them, and we are here today because of what they did." The whole convention center clapped their hands and cheered. "We used to be called the Flawed, but from now on, we are to be called the Freed." And the whole audience cheered once again.

The medals were brought out onto the stage. All three hundred and ten soldiers were honoured. Dar was the first to receive the medal of bravery and then followed the women, and Jenny received a medal, and the young ones received tokens of appreciation. A plaque was installed in the convention center, marking the date on which those once called the Flawed were to be called the Freed. During and after the ceremony, countless people from other areas of the Solar Complex, and outside the boundaries, thanked the soldiers for their gallant efforts. They were all lined up as people shook their hands and then went on to the various festivities.

Towards the end of the night, a few soldiers were left, and they stood around and talked about the honours. As they were talking, one of the soldiers had his amber with him, and it started to vibrate. "Oh no!" he said, as he rushed out of the convention center and shouted, "Elds are coming! Elds are coming!"

Dar ran out of his house, trying to put his armour on. He stopped in the middle of the village square and looked around. He could see a small army of Elds coming towards him. They were not yelling war cries but were walking slowly towards the center of town. Other soldiers started to appear with swords glowing and amber vibrating. The Elds walked right up to Dar and never said a word but laid down their swords and weaponry in front of him. As Dar looked at the Elds coming one by one, the swords grew into a big pile of steel in the middle of the town square. When the last Eld laid down the last sword, Dar heard the last clang of metal against metal.

The senior Elds then walked up to Dar and said, "We surrender."

Dar was a little shocked and asked the senior Eld, "Why are you doing this?"

"Two things," he said. "You have reversed the mountain effects on us, and we find it difficult to function. Daily life, we find, is also hard on our minds."

"And what's the other?" Dar asked.

"The GOL, who promised our kind security and riches, has double-crossed us and left us without very much to show for our years of service. But the main reason we come here today is for protection against those aliens and the GOL, for he has hired them to rid the whole land of us and you. A genocide, he wants."

"Okay," said Dar, "but, first, how did you find out about the aliens?" The Elds said nothing. "I do not trust any of you nor the words you have just spoken. The truth, whatever it is, I do not know right now. This may be a trap, who knows, but I am placing all of you under arrest, and you will be staying with the rest of your clan in the jailhouse."

Dar pulled out his glowing purple sword and said to the Elds, "Before you head to the jail cells, you will be emptying all of your silver here in a pile." He gave the command and said, "Let's go." So, one by one the Elds started walking, and as they reached Dar, the Elds emptied all their silver from their various pockets and headed towards the jail.

After that encounter was over and all the weaponry gathered, the great day of celebration met the stark reality that there was a new unknown to fear in the Solar Complex. The large crowds soon disbursed and headed back to their various towns and villages, and the council decided to meet to discuss what to do next.

In the meeting, Dar stepped up and said, "I am reminded of the recent young one's vision. The word given was 'deception.' I do not trust the Elds, and we do not know just how many there are. So, it may be a trap, but it is somewhat concerning that they would surrender. When we showed the sketch of what one of our soldiers saw in the sky to the Elds, they were terrified. I guess they figured they cannot win against this new enemy."

"What about the rest of the soldiers at Mount Hemor? Do we bring them home, now that the Elds have surrendered?" asked the council.

"No," said Dar, "let us not forget the mountain has to be protected at all costs. We cannot do that again—being under siege mentally." He went on, "What I want to know is where these aliens are at this present moment and what are they planning. But all we know is they were headed west."

"Do we plan a mission westward?"

"No," said Dar, "We do not know if they are here at all. They may have just passed by our planet on the way to another one, who knows for sure. I guess we wait until they make a move or contact us. We are helpless really. I say, we close this meeting and carry on until something happens."

Then the door of the council chamber burst open, and a soldier said, "You better come look at this." So, everyone got up and went outside, and up in the sky was a large alien-type ship, which appeared to be slowly moving westward at first and then stopped. Dar told all the soldiers present to sound the alarm and prepare for a code red alert, which meant everyone at the ready.

A small ship then came from the larger one and

slowly approached the small village and landed on the field not too far away. The door of the craft opened, and three large figures stepped out and headed towards the small group of villagers. The aliens handed them a package. They got back on the small craft and boarded the large ship.

"That's weird," said Dar, and he headed back to the council chamber and opened the package. Dar read it, and it contained a single demand: "We are immensely powerful, and with one blast of our weapon your entire village would be devastated. The only thing we want is all your Amber. We will be back in two days to pick it up."

After reading the note, Dar sat back for a moment and said, "Why do they want our amber?"

Alban said, "Let's give it to them."

"What, are you crazy?" said Dar.

"No, not the real stuff, but a fake amber—made out of explosives, like what we used on the mansion expressed Alban."

"Can we make it in two days?" asked Dar.

"I do not see a problem, if there is no objections Let's get to it right away," said Lars.

"Wait a minute, what are you saying?" replied Dar. He continued speaking and said, "Make the explosives look like amber, and if they fall for that, their ship will be compromised by the fake exploding amber?"

"Yes," said Lars. And continued by asking "Are we all in agreement?

Dar, Alban and Lars said yes.

Meanwhile, the large ship hovered about the village for the two days as the Freed made the fake amber deep underground so as to hide their intentions.

"We have to demand something in return," said Dar. "Let's ask for the GOL in return for the amber."

"Agreed." In two days all the amber was ready, with an explosive charge attached.

When the aliens showed up, Dar confronted them and said, "We want the GOL in return for all of our amber. He must pay for the crimes against our people." The three aliens returned to the ship and stayed there, but within a short time, they returned with the GOL.

As they handed him over, Dar was a bit skeptical and looked over the GOL and said I remember you being a lot taller than this and upon further inspection he noticed this GOL was a mechanical hybrid. Dar said immediately he is a fake and The soldiers pulled their swords, and Dar drew his sword and cut the fake GOL in half and Dar discovered the GOL was made out of wires and fake skin and mechanical parts much like a robot. He proceeded to arrest the aliens with no trouble at all. The aliens were locked up in the same jailhouse as the Elds.

Dar went to the small spacecraft and went inside. He discovered the technology in the craft was considerably basic and simple and looking at it, he wondered, how does this fly? He did not know what to expect. It was rather foreign to him. Dar continued looking at a few gauges and said "Looks like they are operating on empty, no wonder they want our amber—they most likely need a power source. Well, that changes things," said Dar. "And that also tells me this big ship is in no better shape either." They left the small ship and returned to the council.

"Is this the best they have?" Dar thought for a moment and continued, "Could this be what the young ones were talking about—the deception—why would they send old junk alien spacecraft? I looked inside the ship, and there were not many moving parts," exclaimed Dar.

Dar turned to a soldier and asked, "Do we have all of the fake amber ready?"

He said, "Yes."

"Well, let us get it here and load it all on this craft, but hide it so they will bring it to the main ship. Then we blow it up," explained Dar. "That might work. Who knows."

"We have to get those aliens out of jail and send them back where they came from," said Lars.

Dar and the soldiers, along with the council, collectively agreed, and the fake amber was hidden away on the small craft. Dar and a few members of the council visited the aliens in jail.

Dar said, "We are not impressed with your kind showing up here in our village, demanding our most precious amber. Just who do you think you are? We should execute every one of you right now," Dar expressed himself. "But we came together and talked it over, and we decided it might be in the best interests of you and ourselves if you just leave our Solar Complex and never come back. So, if you abide by what we demand and talk to your mother ship, I will lead one of you to your craft so you can talk it over with them. What do you think?"

One of the aliens said he would contact the ship. Dar opened the door of the jail cell, and one of them walked out. One of the soldiers escorted him to his craft. After a ten-minute conversation, the aliens agreed it would be best to follow Dar's request, so immediately the rest of the aliens were led on board their ship. It started to hover and slowly made its way back to the opening doors of the mothership. As it entered, the ship's doors closed, and it started to move away. After a moment, Dar and the entire council heard explosions, and the entire ship was destroyed. The whole village also witnessed what had happened, as bits and pieces of the exploded ship fell to the ground and sparked a few small fires. But they were taken care of as the soldiers doused water on them.

Within less than one hour, the whole sky over the Solar Complex was filled with newer style alien spaceships with colourful lights and awesome looking features. The soldiers stood looking up in amazement and saying to each other, "Now we have done it."

Dar said, "We cannot stay on the surface. Let us get all the women, young ones, and our families to the lower levels of the jailhouse. The lowest level would be best." The warning siren was set off, and Dar said, "Let's all get below, with every suit of armour we can muster."

Dar ran to the aviary and immediately wrote a message saying, "We are under attack from a giant alien space force—send reinforcements but guard the mountain with fifty soldiers." He placed the note in a carrier pigeon and flung it into the air and quickly ran to the lower levels. As he was running, a blast from one of the ships cut down a massive tree that stood in the middle of the village square, and sparks flew everywhere as the tree fell to the ground with a crash of branches. There was much hustle as the last of the Freed went underground.

At the tenth level, all doors were securely closed and barred. The Eld prisoners were just looking at the soldiers hurrying to and fro. They asked, "What's the matter?"

"Aliens, by the thousands, in the sky."

"What are you going to do now?" they asked.

"I do not know," said Dar, as his sword was glowing purple and the amber vibrating. He said, "Do you have any suggestions?"

"See what they want," suggested one of the senior Elds.

Dar said, "I know exactly what they want."

"And what's that?" said the Eld.

"My head," said Dar, "We played a bad joke on them."

As Dar explained what he'd done, the senior Eld said to Dar, "You're finished!"

"Now we are all in the same situation," said Dar, "just how many Elds are out there, anyway?"

"Firstly," said the senior Eld, "we were at a point with the GOL where we were going to revolt against him, but you Flawed found the Book of Secret Knowledge and the three keys. That was the beginning of our downfall. Then, to add insult to injury, you acquired the suits and the purple swords. We knew we were finished, so we tried to take the cave with everything we had. But the amber, along with the swords, were too much for us."

"You haven't answered my question," said Dar. "How many Elds are left in the whole Solar Complex?"

The senior Eld stepped up, came to the jail cell bars and said, "How many do you need?"

Dar said, "About ten thousand."

The senior Eld said, "Outside the Solar Complex,

we have over ten thousand, but it's a week's journey to get here."

Dar said to the Eld, "Up on top, the sky is filled with aliens, and they have started to blast our village. It will be destroyed again." Dar thought for a moment and asked the senior Eld "If you have ten thousand Elds, then why did you lose at Mount Hemor?"

"We were almost there. We were less than an hour away with our whole ten thousand, then, whatever you did in the cave caused us to lose our ability to function. To tell you the truth, for us to be effective, you will have to reverse what you did to us so we can fight against the aliens. Right now, our minds are not doing very well."

"Yes," said Dar, "we know all about that. Eventually, I will have to make that trip to the mountain to see what's going on." As he finished talking to the senior Eld, the lights on the lower tenth level started to flicker and flicker. Dar was very curious and started to make his way to the big, vaulted doors and slowly made his way up to the top. As he walked closer and closer, he could hear strange sounds, then a blast.

When Dar could see what was happening on the surface, he realized the aliens were decimating every house in the village. Then, for a moment, the laser stopped blasting and another small ship, which looked not at all like the other pieces of junk that came before, landed in the middle of what used to be the town square. The GOL himself stepped out, threw a canister on the ground, and left in his spacecraft. Then all the ships left the sky over the Solar Complex village.

Dar ran to the lower level and told everyone, "They are gone." Soon all the people of the village were on top again to pick up the pieces, and once again they feel defeated and overcome with grief and would have to start the long process of rebuilding. Dar said to the women and the remaining soldiers, "It is not safe on top, because we do not know if an alien ground invasion will take place, so gather all the food and supplies you can, and get below to the lowest level."

Dar walked to where the canister was and picked it up. He twisted the top off and inside was a scroll that read, "To all of the inhabitants of the village of the Solar Complex, leave or be blasted to the outer limits. Release the Elds, you Flawed. I want you gone! I will have the mountain back, and you will be FLAWED once again! I did not like what you did to my mansion, so I guess one good turn deserves another." Dar rolled up the scroll and brought it to the council members, and they discussed what to do.

The council met in the lower level of the jailhouse, where the Elds were behind bars. Dar and some of the soldiers were in attendance. A council member took out the scroll and said to the Elds, "We have just received this from your old pal, the GOL."

"What does it say?" asked the senior Eld, as they all stood up and came to the bars.

"Okay," said the council, "here it is." He unfolded the note and showed it to the Elds through the bars.

"That sounds like him," said the Elds, after reading the GOL's words.

"So, what do you think?" asked Dar, unhappy at needing the Elds' help but seeing no other option

"Well, for one thing, we will not have him controlling us anymore. Looks like he wants the whole Solar Complex to himself, so he can use us to mine his silver. We are right back where we started. He does not keep his promises. He only cares about himself." said the senior Eld.

"I guess he wants an answer. What will we tell him?" replied Dar.

The senior Eld spoke up and said, "Tell him we will fight him and his aliens."

"What!" said Dar.

The Elds said, "You cannot go back to being the Flawed now that you have experienced true freedom. It's worth fighting for. If you want us to fight, we cannot, because that mountain has to be in a position that is comfortable for you, and it must be comfortable for us."

"A happy medium," said Dar.

"I am sure there is a sweet spot for all, yes," said the Eld.

Dar asked the senior Eld, "Are you willing to help us in the fight against the aliens if we adjust the lever in the mountain cave?"

"Yes," said the senior Eld. Then Dar and the council let the Elds out.

Dar said, "We have to go to Mount Hemor and find that sweet spot." So, the Elds and the Freed walked to the surface and agreed together to fight the aliens and the GOL.

The senior Eld gathered his remaining small army that was locked up in the jailhouse, and the Freed were there to listen to what he had to say. The senior started to speak, as he looked around to see what was left of the village the aliens destroyed. "There is no way out for us, we have to help our enemy, and in return, he has to help us. The GOL has to be crushed once and for all. Are you not tired of being his slave for meagre pouches of silver—I ask you, where did it get us?"

"Not very far," said a few Elds.

Then, the senior Eld spoke up and said, "We are a small group of Elds, but our family is great, therefore we have to send out for help far and wide. The aliens will be back, and unless we fight together, we will always be slaves to that good for nothing GOL." Then the senior Eld gave orders, "Summon our family.

We need their help, so ride hard and get word to them. We do not have much time, so leave right away to all the outposts of the great Solar Complex." Then seven Elds left in different directions, after they obtained horses, to gather the large family for their help.

After that, the senior Eld said to Dar, "We cannot fight with this mind-altering headache and nausea, plus all the other effects. We have to go to Mount Hemor and find the balance, for both our sakes." Dar agreed and the next day they headed off for the mountain, along with young ones and the keys. Dar also brought the Book of Secret Knowledge, but he kept it hidden from the Elds.

When they were about halfway there, they met the one hundred armoured soldiers coming towards them, and they said, "We got the message and are coming to aid you, but why are you coming this way?"

Dar said, "It's a long story, but right now we have to get to the mountain. And, by the way, we have teamed up with the Elds and are united against aliens and the GOL."

Yes sir said the soldiers.

Another thing said Dar, the GOL has teamed up with them and blasted our village. We are heading to the mountain, but you go to the village and help. We have moved to the lower levels of the jailhouse, because we do not know if an alien ground invasion will happen."

"Okay." said the soldiers, and they thanked Dar for bringing them up to speed. Then, they were off.

Dar, the soldiers, and the Elds finally reached Mount Hemor and were greeted by the remaining soldiers. Dar left the Elds and charged the soldiers not to let the Elds inside of the cave. He privately gathered the young ones at the table and placed the Book of Secrets and went through the steps to move the lever into a desirable position. The three young ones, along with Dar, with his sword and amber, proceeded to move the lever one-quarter of a turn. Dar felt a slight pain in his forehead. He ran out to the front of the cave and asked, "Is that any better?"

The Elds said, "Just slightly better," but the Freed soldiers were not doing so good.

He ran back to the lever and said, "That's not good." He took hold of the lever again and pulled it into the halfway position, between the Flawed and the opposite end slightly. His pain left. He breathed a sigh of relief and ran out to the Elds and asked, "Is that okay?"

They said, "That is much better."

Dar went back in and said, "I think we have found the sweet spot." He proceeded to gather up the book and the keys. He placed them back in his vest. On his way out of the cave, he said to the soldiers guarding it, "Nobody goes in this cave."

"Yes, sir," replied the soldiers.

Dar walked toward the senior Eld and said, "Do we have an agreement?" The Eld turned towards Dar and held out his hand in a good gesture, and they shook. Dar said, "We have to sign that scroll, put it back in the canister, and leave it for that troublemaker. We will tell him we are not abiding by his demands." So, the small group headed back to the battered village.

Along the way, they could see shadows of alien spaceships through the canopy. As they continued walking, Elds came from different directions by the thousands. Over the next three days, the Elds gathered to full capacity, at over ten thousand. Dar could not believe his eyes, and his sword and armour were glowing and vibrating constantly. He said, "This canopy has been a great cover for us. I believe we should hide you Elds in the forest, so that the GOL has no idea you are here. And another thing—he has no idea of the pact that we have made." All the senior Elds agreed and prepared to dig in and get ready in the forest.

Meanwhile, Dar retrieved the canister with the demands and brought it to the Elds. He rolled it out and signed it, and it read, "We declare war upon the GOL and his aliens." Dar signed it on behalf of the Freed, and the senior Eld also signed. But, as he was leaving, Dar slipped another private note into the canister, without the Elds knowing. Then Dar rolled it up and left it in the middle of the village square.

Within one hour, the GOL landed his ship. The

ship's steps lowered, and as the dust settled, he retrieved the canister and opened it right there, as Dar and the Elds secretly watched from the jailhouse's main level. The GOL shook his fist at the jailhouse and said, "If it's a war you want, we will bring it." He ripped up the scroll and threw the canister at the jailhouse, but he noticed another note fall as he walked towards the ship. He stopped, picked it up and read it, and then he left.

Later that night, Dar contacted the GOL privately by secretly delivering messages by a third party. Dar asked him, "What do you want anyway? Why don't you just go away, to the planet from where you came from."

The GOL responded with "I was doing fine here until you stole my book, which led to this mess."

"How long were you going to keep this up—the mountain, and using the Elds for your mining operation?" asked Dar.

"As long as I could."

"Well," said Dar, "it's over."

"No," said the GOL, "it's only the beginning. I made a deal with those aliens, and they want to be compensated."

"Like the Elds?" replied Dar.

"Yes, like the Elds."

"It won't work," said Dar, "we will never go back to the way it was. We are Freed now, and we have come to enjoy it. It is worth fighting for. We will not be Flawed ever again."

The GOL said, "Is that all you have to say?"

"Yes," said Dar, "freedom is worth fighting for."

"We will see," said the GOL.

Dar wrote another message to the GOL, "One more question—why are you doing this?"

"Because," said the GOL, "I want it all." Then the messages stopped coming.

10

TOO MANY ELDS

DAR WALKED TO THE LOWER LEVEL OF THE JAIL-house and retired to his makeshift living quarters. There, the Book of Secret Knowledge and the keys, along with his suit of armour, which he had taken off, rested at his bedside. As he began to fall asleep, he thought about the aliens and the GOL, and the events that had taken place over the past little while. The events and the stress had finally caught up with him. He was exhausted. He thought about the ten thousand Elds in position and ready in the woods, then his eyes opened very wide, and he got up fast.

"Ten thousand Elds," he said to himself, "what have I done?" He tried to rationalize his thoughts, but the more he thought about it the more on edge he felt. Then, a sudden shock of reality—his mind flashed back to one of the young ones saying, "deception." He lay back down with an uneasy feeling, but he was tired, and his mind and body needed rest. As he was going to sleep, he said to himself, "Something is not right." Then he drifted back to sleep.

During his sleep, his active mind and imagination played havoc on him. He dreamt of a takeover by the Elds. In his wild dreaming, he saw himself getting up from his rest and sitting by the edge of his bed, and to his horror, the Book of Secret Knowledge was gone, along with the vest, and his armour, sword, and amber. in a panic state, he quickly rushed to the jail cell doors to find they were locked. He shook the bars, and they opened. He rushed to the top and found the soldiers were all gardening and picking weeds in the village, but the weeds kept growing, and they could not pick them fast enough. He saw their armoured suits had dust all over them, and the swords had been used to chop firewood and had lost their edges. The glow was gone—he rushed over to the suits and searched for the amber, but it was also gone.

"Somebody has stolen the amber!" he shouted. "Where is everybody?" he shouted again.

One of the soldiers replied, "They have all gone to Mount Hemor with the senior Elds and the young ones, to tell stories out of the Book of Secret Knowledge. Some of the soldiers have also gone with their suits, to listen to the Elds."

Then Dar woke up, in sweaty horror, to a dark cell. He reached immediately for the book and found it in the dark, and he found comfort when he found the sword. He lay back down with a great sigh of relief but could not forget about the nightmare. He stumbled to the cell door, made his way up to the top, and went outside to see the activity of Elds mingling with soldiers. He was looking and thinking about his dream. He called on Lars, and the two sat down in a safe place. Dar told him about his dream.

"That's vivid," said Lars and was alarmed at what he was told. "Let us get to the young ones secretly and reveal what you have been given. I think it's a wake-up call," said Lars. So, the two very stealthily made their way to the young ones. They sat in the lower level of the jailhouse, where Dar retold his dream.

The young ones, after listening, said, "You have been given a message—basically we are getting complacent, and what was once our enemy has now become our so-called friend. We opened our borders and compromised the mountain, so they are on the same level playing field. We no longer have the advantage as they did on us for generations."

"As for the aliens," remarked one of the young ones, "just when are they going to attack? It's been over a week now, and there is nothing."

"Do not forget about our last vision."

"Yes," said Dar, "it was 'deception.'" He pondered for a moment, then got up and thanked the young ones. He left with a clearer understanding of what was revealed to him in the dream.

Dar met with the rest of the council and the soldiers, to give a speech in the underground cell where no Elds were permitted. He shared his vision and said, "We cannot let our guard down against the Elds. For the most part, we do not know them. They are supposed to aid in the fight against these so-called aliens, who have failed to make themselves known, yet we have ten thousand Elds here in the middle of our Solar Complex—think about it. What are your thoughts?" asked Dar.

One soldier said, "Our swords and amber are active all the time because of the interaction with the Elds—it's getting annoying."

"I know," said Dar, "they are doing their job."

Alban said, "Maybe these Elds should stay in the woods until this alien thing starts to manifest."

"That's a good idea," said Dar, "We have to be separate from this."

Immediately after the meeting, a notice went out to the Elds, which did not go over too well. The senior Elds called another meeting, including the Freed. At the meeting, Dar presented himself and explained it was best to separate, because of the vibrating amber and the glowing swords.

"It's our defence system," said Dar.

"But we are not at war," said the senior Elds.

"I know," said Dar, "and let us keep it that way. This needs to be done for our sake and yours, and that's all there is to it."

"Okay." agreed the Elds, and they made their exit into the woods. The soldiers' amber stopped vibrating, and the swords stopped glowing. The soldiers were relieved, and Dar felt one hundred percent better.

A few days passed, and the Elds' encampment was getting depleted of food and supplies, and the living conditions in the woods were getting bad—as could be expected with ten thousand Elds living, and waiting, in the woods. They expected the alien fight would be happening by now, but it was very silent. Some of the Elds were not too happy with Dar for making them exit their village. A few fights had broken out between the younger Elds and a few soldiers, and heated words were spoken almost leading to a confrontation, as some swords were glowing purple.

The senior Elds had just about had it with Dar and his decision to relocate them to the woods, and he called him out. The senior Eld said to one of the Freed soldiers, "We are not doing this anymore." So, the soldier went and told Dar about the situation.

Dar thought for a moment and said to the soldier, "Quickly, we haven't got much time. Go to the aviary, and get five pigeons, and bring them back here as fast as you can." While the soldier was gone, Dar wrote on five pieces of paper. The soldier returned very promptly with the birds, and Dar attached the messages to the rings on the birds' legs. He said to the soldiers, "Here, place these birds, each of you, in your vest pockets, and have them ready to fly if things do not go as planned when we meet with these Elds. Don't worry, I have a plan."

"Okay." said the soldiers, and they made their way to the woods where the Elds were staying. Upon arrival, they could feel the tension in the air, as the Elds' mood had changed considerably. The senior Eld came from his makeshift tent and started to say to Dar, "What kind of operation is this? We are here, and you are doing a lot better than us."

Dar said, "I feel we have been fooled again by the GOL and his tactics. I do not see any aliens and—those we did see—are they really against us? Who knows?"

The senior Eld said to Dar, "What prevents us from taking over everything? We are ten thousand strong, and your small army has only two hundred, maybe."

Dar stepped up to the senior Eld, as he took the pigeon out of his vest pocket, and told him, "If I let this bird go, it's going to fly directly to Mount Hemor, and it has a message attached." He asked the five soldiers to back up and bring out the birds from their vests. He told them to spread out and get ready to release them. Dar asked the remaining soldiers, whose swords were glowing, to be ready. Then he turned to the Elds and asked, "Do you want to read the message I have attached to these birds?"

The senior Eld said, "You are bluffing."

Dar took the message from the bird's leg and tossed it to the senior Eld. He immediately opened it and read, "Turn the lever to the Elds' position immediately when you get this message. Signed, DARIUS."

Dar said, "You have enjoyed the peace from your troubled minds these past few weeks, and now you find yourselves not too happy with the current situation. I am not happy either, so what will it be? Do you want to go back to the way you all were? We own the mountain now, and if you do not cooperate, the lever is going back to where it was, and we will resume being enemies." Dar stood his ground and remained silent.

The senior Eld pulled back his strong stance and said, "So it's a lever? Hmmm." He thought for a minute and said, "No, we do not want that for our nation, as you are well aware."

"Are we good then?" asked Dar.

"As good as it can be," said the senior Eld. But Dar felt mistrust had entered the hearts of both parties.

On the way back to the village, one of the soldiers said to Dar, "Are these birds trained to fly to Mount Hemor?"

"No," said Dar, as he laughed in relief, "they do not have a clue where Mount Hemor is." The soldiers just laughed, and Dar said, "there was only one bird trained, and it's there at Mount Hemor. I had to do something. These Elds are getting restless. We might have to ratchet the lever up to the Elds' position if they continue this pattern."

When Dar arrived back at the village, he met with the council. He spoke a dire warning and said the Elds are not at all happy. He also said they must train some new pigeons immediately, to go to and from Mount Hemor, for an emergency scenario.

Dar said, "We must get some young ones out there at the cave, along with some of the women, and especially Jenny, for support. They will also need the book and keys. We cannot turn that lever without the young ones."

"Yes, good idea," agreed the council.

Dar said, "I feel the Elds are up to something. I do not trust them. The alien invasion we figured was going to happen has gone silent, and I have to let you know, I talked with the GOL the other night, just to try and persuade him to leave this planet."

Alban said, "That was a big risk!"

"Yes, I know, but I thought he would listen to reason and hoped he would come around."

"What did he say?" asked Alban.

"He said, 'I want it all.'"

A moan was heard from the council. "We have to

rid our Solar Complex of this character, once and for all," said Dar. "I also think it's best that we ask the Elds to leave our forest and go back to where they came from, and to wait for the call to war with the aliens—if that is ever going to happen. But first, we set up the young ones at Mount Hemor. We need to get them there as soon as possible, for I think we do not have much time. We also need to train as many pigeons as we can to fly back and forth from Mount Hemor and set up another aviary in another part of the Solar Complex, just in case. Please, I say," said Dar, "you all have to keep this very secret, and the trip to Mount Hemor has to begin tonight." All the council agreed with Dar's plan.

The next day, the soldiers were busy with the birds. Dar gave instructions to some of the women, including Jenny, because she was at the mountain before and knew what to do with the books and the three keys. The women and children slipped out under the cover of darkness. A note was sent along with them, written by Dar to the soldiers at the cave, with detailed plans. It was also a coded message just in case something went wrong on the journey.

Dar was busy managing the new mission and asked the soldiers to contact him immediately when everything was ready to go. In the meantime, Dar tried as best he could to keep the peace between the Elds and the Freed, but he could tell the situation was getting more strained by the day. He was rushing the soldiers to see if some of the birds had returned with the message.

"We will let you know as soon as possible."

Dar thought to himself, "I need to buy some time." So, he loaded some of the larger carts with food for the Elds and delivered them to the woods. The Elds were somewhat grateful, and he felt he had appeased them, but for how long he was not quite sure. He knew it was getting to a point where the tension would be too much.

Dar made a few more trips in the coming days and asked the senior Elds, "Let me know what I can do for you, and we will try our best to accommodate." The next day, word came from one of the pigeon trainers to say the test flight was a success. Within a few more hours, all the birds had made it back.

Dar told them, "Take half of the birds to another location, and get a message ready that says, 'Turn the lever to the Elds' position immediately when you get this message, signed DARIUS.'" So, all the trained birds had the message attached to their legs and were waiting at the aviary. Then, within a few days, word came that the group with the young ones had reached Mount Hemor.

Then Dar met with the council and confirmed that everything was ready.

"Great," said the council, "now we can get these Elds out of our woods."

Dar said, "I will handle it." He got all the soldiers

in uniform, and they made their way to the Elds in the forest. The senior Eld saw Dar coming, as the amber vibrated, and the swords started to glow.

"What's this?" asked the senior Eld, as the other Elds started to crowd the area.

Dar replied, "We do not have many supplies left, and our resources are getting depleted."

"What do you suggest?" asked the senior Eld.

"We think it best if you return to your land to get replenished."

"That's a good idea," agreed the senior Eld, but the look on his face said anything but. He turned around and said out loud, "If that's the way you want it, then we will leave."

Dar said, "This alien thing, I think it's not going to happen." He paused a moment and then added, "It would have happened by now."

The senior Eld said, "We will be gone in the morning."

Dar said, "Great, that's best for all." He turned to leave with the soldiers who held the glowing purple swords.

That night, Dar was rather restless after the confrontation, when a soldier came running to the cell where he was staying and said to him, "There is activity in the woods—some bright light—and a figure came out of it. I had a closer look, and it was the GOL—he met with the Elds."

"My suspicions were right," said Dar, and he quickly jumped up and sounded the alarm. He got up to the top as fast as he could and could see thousands of Elds coming through the woods, running and holding swords of their own.

Dar shouted as loud as he could, "Release the birds—Release the birds as fast as you can!" The soldiers ran and opened the cages, and the birds began to fly, but they were knocked out of the sky. Dar saw this and said to the soldiers, "Run—you and three others—to the other aviary, and release the birds! Go!" One of the soldiers, as he was running, was struck and killed by a flying object, but the other three faded into the night. Dar hoped they would reach the aviary in time.

The Elds were upon the village by the thousands and thousands. The soldiers were not prepared for the mad rush of Elds and were in various stages of fighting, as silver spilled all over the ground. Dar sang out loudly, "Let's get to the jailhouse." But there was no time. The entrance was heavily guarded by the Elds. Dar shouted at the soldiers, "Retreat into the woods. There are just too many of them."

Under the cover of the night, all they could see were glowing swords and amber, as they ran until no Elds were chasing them. After running a fair distance, they were exhausted and took a rest by the edge of the river. One of the soldiers said, "I never saw that coming."

"I did," said Dar, as he was catching his breath and

said, "I have been mentally preparing for this very situation for awhile, but I did not know when it was going to happen. I have been feeling uneasy about the Elds living alongside us. My gut was right," said Dar. "I knew it!"

"What do we do now?" asked one of the tired soldiers.

Dar answered, "We have to hold out until the message sent by the carrier pigeons is received at Mount Hemor. It should take them about two hours to fly there. It will take a short time to get the book opened and for the young ones to get positioned, along with the soldiers, to turn that lever to the Elds' position."

"I knew we could not trust them," said one of the soldiers.

"I hear you," said Dar, "but now we have to wait in the woods until the lever is pulled. There are just too many of them to fight. Right now, they are not bothered by the mountain. It is in the neutral position, so they are strong, and we must wait until morning. In the meantime, we must get a good night's rest for tomorrow. We may have to fight to the death if that lever is not turned. Let us hope that the young ones have initiated the mountain, and it starts working for us again."

As the night approached, not a word was heard in the forest but crickets and the slowly rippling river. All ears were peeled. Suddenly, the group heard a small party of Elds. They were searching for the Freed, but the Freed were ready and surprised the Elds. They found it rather difficult, and the fighting took longer than usual to defeat them.

Finally, the last Eld dropped, and the silver fell to the ground. The soldiers remarked that the Elds were getting stronger.

"No," said Dar, "the mountain has not yet been activated. We have to wait a little while longer." No sooner had they won the victory than another test was coming. Just before sunrise, a larger group of Elds started to wage war on the Freed in the middle of their forest. The amber started vibrating, and the swords again glowed purple as the intense fighting started. The Elds had a strong number, and the fight was so fierce that many of the soldiers became weary with fatigue. Some were killed, and others fell in exhaustion.

When it looked like all was lost, Dar noticed the Elds were starting to feel the effects of the mountain. He could see their heads bothered them and knew something was working. The Freed, then, were freed and no longer neutral. They were empowered, and the Elds were weakened, so the exhausted soldiers found a little burst of energy when Dar shouted, "The mountain is activated!" They defeated the onslaught of attacking Elds.

After the battle, the soldiers found some rest, and Dar said, "What would we have done if the young ones, or the birds for that matter, never reached the mountain? I figured for a moment there we were done for. There were just too many Elds."

After a breather, one of the soldiers said, "What now?"

Dar told them, "We get our fallen soldiers and bring them home for a proper burial. I figure the Elds are gone from our village and our territory. They know they have been defeated. The mental toll has taken place by now, and they are the new Flawed once again. Let us get ready, pack it up, and make our way back home."

11

THE ALIEN BASE

AFTER QUICKLY REFRESHING THEMSELVES IN THE river, the soldiers got ready and made their way out from the deep forest. The walk was quiet as they strolled along on the green mossy path with the rippling river beside them. The sun was bright, but the canopy of the very tall trees blocked most of it out. Dar thought, as he walked along the path, "We have another victory under our belt." But, in the back of his mind, he was still worried about the GOL. The closer they got to the village, the more they could see the disaster caused by the aliens, plus the mess the Elds left. As they walked, there was no other trace of the Elds. When they finally arrived in the village, one of the soldiers said, "Back to square one."

Dar said, "Tomorrow, we need to get to Mount Hemor and check out the situation there. We will thank the young ones and the women soldiers for a job well done, for without them, we would most likely have lost that fight."

That night, the soldiers were licking their wounds and resting. The next morning, they retrieved the bodies of the deceased soldiers—their friends. They were wrapped for the journey home, some had a few stories about their bravery, but nobody was in the mood to talk about death. No sooner had they arrived in the village than they prepared for another journey to Mount Hemor to get their bearings and check on where things stand.

After preparations were made, they were off again on another trip through the deep forest. It was uneventful and somewhat boring after the recent turmoil. There were no signs of any Elds peeking through the leaves or in the trees, not even hiding behind rocks. They finally reached the mountain's entrance, which was guarded by Freed soldiers, who were happy to see new faces, for they had been gone a long time since the great turnover of power. The young ones came running with Jenny close to their side, and the women soldiers greeted Dar and the others. They all had great conversations, and everyone was brought up to speed on the past few excursions.

After all the talking was done, they checked out the mountain. They had a little time to relax, and some of the men looked up at the mountain and said, "Who wants to climb this thing?" A few young soldiers who were game for anything decided to go to the top. They were gone for about two hours, but after the trip to the top, they returned and urgently sought out Dar. They spoke to him and told him of the objects they had spotted.

"It's something we think you should see."

"What is it?" asked Dar.

"A silver craft, shining in the sun just northeast of here."

"Okay," said Dar, "I guess I've got to climb this thing." So, he prepared himself and started the climb with the others. When they reached the top again, the view was spectacular, and Dar could see for miles. When he looked to the northeast, he could see the alien spacecraft, with its silvery body shining in the sun. Dar took out his monoscope and had a closer look, then the other soldiers took turns looking as well.

"What are we going to do with that?" one of the soldiers asked anxiously. They all sat for a moment and thought.

Dar said, "I bet they are thinking they have us for sure. But what if we took the fight to them and surprised them? Sabotage their craft, vandalize everything, destroy it so it cannot fly. If it cannot fly, it cannot blast our village. We cannot wait, we must act."

One soldier said, "Remember the amber cubes that exploded with the last old spaceship they had? If we had some more of them, that might make this trip worthwhile. I bet you're going to say we have to ride back to the village..."

"No," said Dar, "we send a message by the pigeons—it's all set up—we send a message by the birds to get the soldiers to make two hundred exploding cubes."

"Yes, that's a great plan. Get the birds ready!"

"Let us get three birds ready, just in case something happens to one. In the meantime, we wait here for them to arrive. To tell you the truth," said Dar, "I am getting tired of travelling."

The birds were made ready, with messages attached, and released. Dar said, "We have the element of surprise on our side, but I want a soldier here at all times on top of this mountain, watching those ships and looking with this scope. The element of surprise is no good if we are spotted, so I want one soldier on the top as the lookout and another soldier midway down to relay the warning. If something is coming at us, we need to know so we can get into the cave and shut the doors, so our cover will not be blown. You, on the mountain, will have to hide. While we are waiting, we need to hunt for some extra meat and get ready for that trip. I am delegating these tasks to volunteers; you guys can handle it. It is about twenty-five miles from here. Fill all the water jugs by the river and feed the horses as well. I am going to check on things in the caves to ensure everything is fine, especially the Eld lever. But the Elds are the least of our worries now."

After securing the cave, and making sure there were no loose ends, Dar had a good look at the soldiers and found they were looking very tired. He thought for a moment of the recent fighting and travelling back and forth to the village and the mountain. He spoke to them and said, "While we are waiting for the cubes, and before we start our next expedition to that alien base, I want you to catch up on some relaxation. I do not know when we will next have a chance to get some rest. So, for the next little while, just rest up until we get that shipment. But I still want that mountain top guarded and to keep an eye on those ships."

At the end of the few days' rest, a pigeon flew in with a message attached to its legs, which read, "Cubes ready to be delivered. Will get them there as fast as we can."

Dar announced the news to the soldiers, and he said, "That still gives you three to five days more relaxation time, so enjoy it." As the soldiers rested, they kept guard over the mountain. One day there was a shout from on the top of the mountain, which was repeated by another soldier halfway down the mountain. When it finally reached the cave, it said, "Alien ship is moving our way."

Dar called out, "Everybody into the cave." And it was repeated to the midpoint and the top. Soldiers were running everywhere, gathering swords and suits as fast as they could and running to the cave. The soldiers on the mountain took cover as the alien ship slowly passed over the mountain. It abruptly stopped for a moment and hovered over the cave opening, which was closed with everyone deep inside. It left the area and headed northeast again.

Dar said, "I wonder, did it see anything? That was a close one." He opened the cave door, and at the entrance, he saw a small article of clothing. He picked it up and thought for a moment, "Is our cover blown?" He showed the soldiers, who said nothing because they were caught unawares. "I guess we will assume they have seen this, but we do not know for certain."

One soldier said, "They may know we are here, but they do not know that we know where they are."

"Good point," said Dar, "So I guess we are still planning to bomb them. Let us keep this article of clothing right where it lies, because if they come again and it's gone, they will know someone is here." That night, Dar could not help but wonder if he was leading his soldiers into a trap. The hovering craft was bothering him. He could not sleep, so he got up and went outside the cave. It was midnight, and the stars were all out, and it was a full moon.

He sat for a while, and another soldier came out and sat down. He said, "I was a little worried about the craft that hovered over our cave."

"Yes," said Dar, "I was too. I came out here to get some air—I could not sleep—what if they saw something? Are we walking into a trap? I do not know what to do now." He pondered the question as the full moon lit up the midnight sky. He thought to himself, "Do the young ones have any new visions? That would certainly be helpful. But we cannot wake them now, I will wait for the morning." Dar decided to finally turn in for the night and closed the cave door.

Up early, the next day, Dar could hardly wait to see if one of the young ones received a word or something to help ease his mind. He visited the women soldiers and asked one of them if they heard anything. "One of the young ones mentioned something in her sleep, but we could not make any sense of it." Dar asked that soldier if she would pay a little bit more attention tonight, and maybe move a little closer just in case the young one reveals something. "Yes, I will do that," she said.

But for most of the day, they continued to watch the alien base from the mountain. The soldier on top of the mountain took out the scope and had a closer look around the area. He noticed a figure moving at the base of the mountain. He did not shout, but quickly headed to the midpoint and spoke quietly to the soldier there. "We have company at the base of the north mountain. Go tell Dar but keep very quiet." The second soldier hurried down the mountain and ran into the cave. He told Dar about the figure at the base of the north mountain.

Dar left immediately and gathered the soldiers. He said, "Four of you go west, and four of us will go east, and whoever catches him, bring him back to the cave for questioning." So, they set out around the mountain very quietly and stealthy, walking slowly and looking very carefully. The other team did the same in the opposite direction. No sooner had they set out than they found the figure with his horse. That gave him away, with all the noise horses make. The figure was hiding behind a large rock.

Dar said, "Give it up, we know you are there." The figure appeared, and it was an alien. Dar drew his sword and approached the alien, then, from out of nowhere, the small craft hovered above them. There was a bright beam of light, and the alien ran deeper into the woods without his horse. As the alien ship continued shining its light, they all followed and tried to catch it, but it was fast, and they were running hard. Then, the alien ship moved with incredible speed and landed in a field on the edge of the woods. As they broke out of the woods, they could see the ship lowering its stairs, and the alien ran to it and climbed the stairs. It stopped halfway up and looked at them, and then it boarded. The stairs closed, and the ship shot into the night sky. All they could hear then was silence and crickets chirping in the darkness.

They all sat down in the field, exhausted. "Who knew aliens could run that fast," Dar said. As they caught their breath, Dar said sadly, "We have been found out. They know we are here." They headed back to the cave, gathered together, and pondered it all again.

"What are we going to do? They know we are here for sure. We still have two days before our cubes arrive. Let us hope those aliens do not start a war with us." Dar thought for a moment.

"Do we move from here, now that we have been found out?"

"Yes," he said, "we cannot stay here, it's unsafe. We must pack up everything and move close to the soldiers with the cubes. At least we will be a day's journey from this place. The element of surprise is still on our side, if the aliens come to the mountain and we are not here."

"Yes, that's it! Let us get ready to meet our soldiers a day ahead of time, then move in another direction, to catch them unawares. Hopefully, they will not find us. Don't forget to leave that piece of clothing by the outside of the cave, where it was the last time they came."

So, they packed it all up and headed to meet the other soldiers. One of the women, who was listening to the young one the previous night, spoke to Dar as they were riding through the forest. She said she overheard the young one talking in her sleep again, "Red swords, red swords, there will be a great reward."

Dar said, "What does that mean?"

"Beats me," said the woman, "I only repeat what I hear."

After travelling for a day, the soldiers reached the other soldiers coming from the village. They asked, "Why are you meeting us?"

"We have had a change of plans—the aliens know that we were at the mountain," said Dar, "so we left there yesterday and have not seen them since."

"Our plan now," said Dar, "is to go around, approach from the west, and make our way northeast to where they are located. So, hopefully, they do not send scouts out, but I fear they will be looking for us." Then he asked, "Was there any trouble with the cubes?"

"No," said a soldier from the village, "everything went according to plan, just like the last time."

"Good," said Dar. "Let's move." And they travelled on through the forest. Dar asked if the few days of rest were helpful.

"Yes," said the group, "but we are a little bit nervous about fighting aliens."

"Well," said Dar, "if we can deliver the cubes, we might win without having to go hand-to-hand in combat." As they got closer to the alien base, they could see spacecraft going to and fro.

"We have to wait until nighttime," explained Dar. "Right now, we stand out. It's only because of the canopy hiding us so far that we are safe."

Finally, night came, and the soldiers prepared to

place the amber cubes on the ships. but as they peered out of the edge of the woods, they saw the alien ships were closely guarded by many aliens, still on duty. The group retreated to the woods again and said, "That's near impossible—we will be seen for sure."

Dar said, "I figured these creatures would sleep. What are we going to do now? We cannot rush them. There are too many, and we do not know how many of them are on the base—maybe thousands—we would be sitting ducks. I feel we must retreat. We cannot face them on their turf—we have no idea what they are capable of. We do not know what kind of weapons they have or what their weapons can do. We just cannot raid them; I feel it would be suicide. Let us pull back and head home and come up with another plan. What do you think? Am I wrong to be cautious?"

The soldiers all agreed and said, "We have a bad feeling about this too."

"Okay," said Dar, "let us get out of here." Then, everyone got on their horses and rode back to the village over a three-day journey.

When the group finally got back home, Dar approached the council and told them about the deceased (soldiers) and the awesome challenge they were faced with now.

"It could not be breached," said Dar, "the base was

too large, and we did not know how many were there. The ships were always guarded. I did not want to put our soldiers in harm's way. It would be the end of our way of life and mean death for most of us. The other soldiers had a bad feeling about the whole idea as well. I am sorry, but I am at my wit's end. I do not know what to do next."

The council spoke together and said to Dar, "I guess we wait."

"Yes, but wait for what?" wondered Dar. "Well, I think we should all be underground from now on, until we figure out what to do."

"Yes," said the council, "we can all agree on that." So, the word was sent out to hide underground from fear of an alien invasion that could happen at any time.

Dar was a little worried and had doubts about the chances of winning a fight against the aliens. "They have ships with blasters, we have swords. What chance do we have?" He wondered, as he sat in the lower level of the jailhouse. He was thinking hard and then realized the cave was not protected. He thought about that in a sort of panic, but thought, "Without the book and the keys, the Elds have no chance of reversing the lever." That night he did not get much sleep but kept trying to figure out what to do with the GOL and the aliens. Finally, out of exhaustion, he fell asleep.

A knock came on his cell door the next morning. It was a soldier who had been on the night watch. He said, "The GOL left you another message. He landed and left the canister in the middle of the town square, just like before."

"Great," Dar said, and he made his way up to the surface. Up top, he walked slowly over to the canister and picked it up. He did not open it but delivered it to Lars and the rest of the council, and asked Lars to read the message.

The council member unscrewed the top and pulled out the scroll. It read, "I want all of my silver returned, and the rest of the things that were in my mansion. This time you will comply."

"Well, that about sums it up," said Dar.

"What do you think?" asked Lars, the council member.

"If he wants it, he is going to have to come and take it. We are not giving it to him. I like the feeling of being free. Our village has been freed—my parents know me, and they have a full memory now—no more Darkness. Is that worth fighting for? Our children's future cannot be stolen by this GOL character. So, I say, no way, I will fight to the death with everything I have."

"We have to get the soldiers to feel like you do," said Lars.

"It will not be hard," said Dar, "for they are Freed too. Give me that scroll." The leader wrote on it in red letters, "Not a chance," and he slipped the scroll in and screwed on the top. Dar walked back to the middle of the village square with anger, threw it down, and walked away.

He then called for a meeting with all the soldiers and told them what the GOL demanded. The soldiers were upset and angry, and Dar knew he had inspired a strong sense of wanting to fight for their new way of life.

"Okay," said Dar, "tonight the canister will be picked up by one of them and brought back to that character, and he is going to read my little message I wrote to him. He will not be happy."

Later that night, in a miraculous vision, one of the young ones who had the original dream said, "He is still coming, he is still coming."

Gwen relayed the message to Dar, and he said "Who is coming?

"I wish I knew," said Gwen.

Dar sounded a little frustrated. "We certainly need somebody now." As he came out from the young ones' cell and walked to the top, it was nighttime, and he saw the canister had already been retrieved. He put his hands on his head and said to himself, "It won't be long now."

Dar went to the bottom of the jailhouse and prepared as best as he could, checking the suit and making sure the amber was there. He handled his sword and picked up the shield, and he sat down on the edge of his makeshift bed with his head in his hands. Apart from the other troubles on his mind, he was thinking about the deceased soldiers and the tragic loss of family members. He lay down and said, "We have to bury these soldiers with full honours." Then he went to sleep.

The next morning, Dar had the deceased soldiers on his mind, and after a quick breakfast, headed to the council and said, "We have to honour the fallen soldiers."

"Yes," said the council, "with full decoration and medals. Contact their fathers and mothers, and anyone else related to them. Let us do this tomorrow, while it's relatively calm."

"Yes," agreed Dar, as he headed out the door to contact his family. He knocked at the doors of the fallen soldiers' parents' houses and one of the fathers greeted Dar. They were happy to see him, and they invited him in, and they sat down and talked about their son and the funeral arrangements. The soldier's father wondered if he could say a few words at his son's ceremony.

"Yes, I am counting on you. We need to say goodbye and thank him for his service."

The next day, the village was preparing to say goodbye to their sons, daughters and heroes. The Freed flags were at half-staff, and all soldiers were in attendance with full dress. Dar addressed the audience and spoke a little of the struggle, but only said a few words. He called upon one of the fallen soldier's fathers. The soldier's father then proceeded to the podium and began to speak.

He said, "As you know, for the longest time I have not been well. My mind left me about two years ago and I, for the most part, forgot everything. But when Dar and the soldiers conquered the mountain and reversed the Darkness, I came to myself once again. Then one day I found out my son was a soldier, and he had a part in defeating the GOL. If it were not for the bravery of our soldiers, I would have died not knowing the real reason we were kept in the dark all these years. So, I want to thank Len, my son, the soldier, and all the soldiers for making the Flawed, the Freed." He then thanked everybody who showed up to the funeral, and the soldier's mother was asked to come and join her husband at the podium, where they received the Freed flag and the medal of bravery for their son's contribution to the war. The soldier's father and mother stepped down off the stage and proceeded to the gravesite, and the soldiers were lowered into the ground.

A moment of silence was observed and then, out of nowhere, a silver alien ship buzzed the gravesite and the limbs of the trees waved as a whisk of air blew against the audience and dust picked up and clouded the air. Dar looked up in disgust at the dirty deed and spoke. "That was a low blow," as he rushed to the soldiers' fathers and mothers. Dar reassured them, "Their day is coming."

12

THE FIGHT OF
OUR LIVES

SHORTLY AFTER, DAR ADVISED THE REST OF THE village to go underground for safety's sake. But no sooner had Dar spoken the words, than he heard one of the soldiers say, "Here they come."

As he looked up, Dar said to the remaining women and children, "Get to the jailhouse. Stay at the lowest level, and lock all the doors." They hurried the last of them inside, and the soldiers ran for cover amongst the houses and buildings that were not too destroyed by the aliens' last visit. The sky was filled with alien ships, and they began to blast the already tattered houses, the buildings, and the ground. Some of the soldiers were killed as they tried to hide.

Dar said, "Spread the word to head for the forest as fast as you can and see if we cannot get some cover and protection from the canopy." All the remaining soldiers ran for the forest, and the rest of the soldiers saw them and joined them as the aliens blasted the village again. Dar shouted, "I guess we are in it now. At least the canopy gives us cover for the time being."

"What do we do now?" asked one of the soldiers.

"Nothing," said Dar, "how can we fight against blasters and spaceships? Here we are, in the middle of the forest with nothing but swords and shields. Our village just got shot to pieces—we are helpless."

Then a large alien ship hovered over the canopy and a wide laser appeared, then the canopy started to smoke, and the heat generated by the laser caught the canopy on fire. The soldiers retreated and retreated, until there was no more canopy and the forest floor was as bright as day is long.

"We are sitting ducks," said Dar. "Quick, get behind rocks and big trees—jump in the river if you have to—but hide and run for your lives." But the alien space crafts spotted them, and Dar looked up from behind a large rock and watched in amazement as the aliens were winning. He was helpless and could do nothing, and he was getting tired. He dropped his sword and watched as the ships blasted and blasted relentlessly. He slumped down in defeat and was just watching the sky filled with aliens, as the blasters pounded the forest floor and the soldiers ran for cover. As they were hit, they were tossed into the air from the strong blasts.

When Dar figured all was lost, he looked into the sky, and the sun was blocked by another great ship, but this one got his attention, and he was fully awake as he watched it fly towards the other ships. The giant ship sent out what looked like a rippling wave, and it made all the other alien ships lose power. They all fell out of the sky and slowly hovered before landing on the forest floor. Many of the soldiers looked out from behind rocks and trees, and even from under the water, and saw the aliens get out of their broken ships.

At once, Dar's sword, lying in the green grass beside him, began to glow a bright red colour. He took hold of it and got up, and he could see red glowing swords everywhere on the forest floor that was held by his soldiers. There was a moment of complete silence, as all the aliens stood outside of their ships just looking at the soldiers with the red swords. Then Dar came to himself and shouted a deep, blood-curdling yell. "FIGHT," and all the remaining soldiers ran towards the aliens, jumping over rocks and running from behind trees with intent. The aliens sent out small blasts from their handheld devices, but the red glowing swords split the blasts in two, and they never came to anything.

The aliens were rushed by the Freed soldiers and quickly overcome. They tried to retreat and get back into their crafts. Some of them made it, but the crafts had no power and could not start. The soldiers found out the red swords could cut an alien spaceship in two, just by striking it.

Toward the end of the evening, most of the aliens were dead on the forest floor. Some of them escaped into the deep forest. Some of the remaining ships were destroyed by the glowing red swords. When the carnage came to an end, the swords stopped glowing, and the exhausted soldiers just looked around at the forest floor. There must have been two thousand aliens stacked on top of one another, some on the rocks, some in the water and some in the trees.

Dar looked around at who was left, and he managed to count about one hundred and fifty or so soldiers. He said to himself under his breath, "It looks like we lost about half." He looked at his sword and said, "I do not know where this came from." He looked up in the sky, and the giant ship was still hovering. "All I know," he said, "is that, as I looked up at that ship, it sent out a wave that sent all of those other alien ships to the ground." He pointed to them. "Then this sword, which fell out of my hand from exhaustion when I figured we had lost for sure, started to glow red. I saw it as a sign, then I picked it up and looked at the aliens. What else could I say, so I yelled 'FIGHT.' I cannot believe it! We won!"

Remembering their other enemy, Dar turned to the soldiers and asked out loud, "Did anyone see the GOL?"

"No, he is not here," said the soldiers. Then the giant ship in the sky began descending slowly until it landed on the forest floor.

Dar looked to his right and could see the young ones running, along with Jenny, towards the ship. They were singing out, "He is here, he is here." The women followed close behind. Dar remembered the young one's vision about the glowing red swords, and he said, "It's starting to make sense—all these visions and words." The ship came to a full stop on the forest floor, and the door opened and three large alien figures stepped out. A small being, which looked like a young one, appeared and walked down the steps behind them. The young ones ran and gathered around the small being like they were long lost friends. Dar was bewildered at what he was seeing and stood watching in amazement.

The soldiers gathered around him and asked, "What is this?"

"I have no idea," replied Dar.

The women came over to the soldiers and said, "While you were fighting the aliens, the young ones had constant visions that said, 'I am coming, I am coming.' We were too afraid to leave the lower level, for fear of the fight. We figured we were all going to die, and we did not know what to make of the young ones. But, when there was no more fighting, we went to the top, and the young ones just knew and started to run towards that ship."

"What do we do now?"

"Let's go see that being," said Dar. So, the soldiers and the women started to walk towards the ship. The small being then motioned his hand for them to come to him. They did not know what to expect. Then they were there, in front of him and the three tall alien figures, who were just looking at them. The Freed looked at them in confusion. They laid down their swords and armour, and a sense of peace came over them. Then the small being began to speak.

"I have been watching your plight and struggle for a long time and have been wanting to intervene. I am the one who has been sending you messages all these years to encourage you through your young ones. The GOL has managed to weaponize the meteor that landed here many years ago, and that is why you have been called the Flawed. The Elds were his army of miners, and he exploited them, but when that did not work for him, he contacted the outer Solar Complex. That was not allowed, so I had to intervene this time. He had gone too far—he would have killed you all, but you have young ones, and they are dear to me, for I once was a young one. But that is a story for another time," the small being said. "One thing remains. Out in the deep Solar Complex is a colony of the group you have called the Elds, and you have weaponized this mountain against them. Now they are not doing particularly well themselves—they have lost their memories and their fathers and mothers to this terrible curse. You know this feeling well. It looks like you have won this war, but only with my help. Now I am going to balance the whole Solar Complex when I leave. But do not worry, I will continue to send the young ones warnings, if need be, to help you and maybe the Elds."

That was it, the small being said no more. The being hugged the young ones, every one of them, and walked back into the spaceship, along with the three tall figures. It slowly ascended and flew away.

"Wow!" said Dar, "Now we are free. But—" he paused for a moment and asked a question. "Where is that GOL?"

"Who cares," said one of the soldiers, "we have lots of work to do. Our village is shot to pieces, and all those dead aliens must be removed. That will be a huge task."

"Yes, we will have to get on that tomorrow, before they start to stink and foul up the river."

Dar said, "I was touched by the words of that small being."

"How so?" said one of the soldiers.

"We are doing to the Elds what the GOL did to us, now the Elds are losing their families and feeling the effects of the lever. We are no better than the GOL." Dar added, "We need to head out to the mountain again and turn that lever to the neutral position so we both can start living."

"After hearing that small being," said the soldiers, "we feel this is the right thing to do. But first, we must gather our fallen soldiers. They are scattered everywhere on the forest floor. We have to honour them, also, for their gallant effort."

So, after a very strenuous day and night, the Freed finally slept very well, knowing all threats were gone, and at last, they were totally freed from aliens and the Elds and, for now, the GOL. The speech of the small being so impacted the soldiers that they all got up and headed to Mount Hemor.

It took them a while to get there, but they finally neared Mount Hemor after a few days' journey. One of the group members said, "I am sure this is the way I have walked it many times."

"Yes, me too," agreed Dar. But as they came up over the ridge to view the mountain, there was nothing there except a giant crater where the mountain stood. Dar remembered the small being talking about evening the odds—that it was going to do something to balance the Solar Complex. "I guess he did it. No more Mount Hemor, no more using that device against each other. Now," said Dar, "we are both truly Freed."

13

THE FINAL BATTLE

THE SOLDIERS HEADED BACK THROUGH THE forest for the long journey home. When they finally arrived, they discovered the Elds had started to help in the rebuilding of the village. Dar told the soldiers to lay down their swords and greet the Elds, and thank them for helping. The women and the young ones were preparing food and laying it on tables for their once mortal enemies, and they all sat down and ate together in the new peaceful Solar Complex.

The next day, the council met and made plans to rebuild the village. The call once again went out to carpenters and labourers inside and outside of the Solar Complex. They planned another ceremony for the fallen soldiers—all one hundred and fifty. Their suits and swords, along with the amber, were securely locked away, in hopes they would never need them again. The Elds and the Freed were working side by side as they rebuilt the village and cleared the forest of all the dead aliens, which seemed to be taking its toll on the group.

Some of the soldiers took it upon themselves to bring the broken spaceships inside By heavy lifting with horses and carts, they were moved to a secure location in the jailhouse, but in that process, a few of the Freed investigated the components in the ships and managed to wire together some of the devices that were not too severely damaged. They used their amber as a power source and rigged it together by trial and error. They were by no means experts, and by a complete fluke, the device lit up and cast an image on the wall. It was a sector in the Solar Complex, but far away, on the outer edges, and it was marked by a red X. The soldiers who managed to figure out the devices earned the title of techs, and the new found information was important enough that they contacted Dar.

When Dar came in to see what they had found, he was wearing a carpenter's tool belt. The techs explained, "We have managed to piece together some of the components in the alien spaceships, and so far, this is what we have come up with." They gestured to the image projected on the wall.

Dar looked at the red X and said, "That's on the outer edges of the Solar Complex. You know that GOL is still out there. I wonder if he is at the red X. Things are very good right now. Since the mountain is gone, we have peace with the Elds, our families are thriving, the land has returned to normal, and our culture, for the first time in ages, is doing well," explained Dar.

"That red X is bothering me. But is it bothering me enough that I want to go and check it out?" He picked up his hammer from his tool belt and said, "There is much work to be done here, but does that red X mean the GOL is rebuilding? I need more information. See what else you can gather out of these devices and whatever else you can find in those alien spacecraft. Dar turned to one of the techs, whose name was Devon, and he said to him, "Keep me posted on what you find out. Meanwhile, I am rebuilding my house again," said Dar.

Devon said, "Sure thing, Dar," and he ordered the team to gather more devices from various broken spaceships that remained from the carnage, and they worked night and day to find another image or voice messages. "Maybe we are looking in the wrong places," Devon said, "Are there any other compartments in those ships? We have only been concentrating on the devices, I wonder, is there anything written down in a logbook or journal?" Devon ordered the team to check over every ship in its damaged state and tear each and every craft inside out.

As luck would have it, they discovered a logbook with coordinates. Devon and the tech team brought all the info to the lower level and analyzed it over and over before they brought it to Dar. Devon and the techs came to the same conclusion, then they called for Dar. This time when he came, he was wearing a gardening outfit.

The techs looked at him, and he said, "My lady friend likes flowers, is that okay?"

Devon spoke up and said, "We have found something else. We did as you said, and we searched inside and out in those ships. We found logbooks and recorded messages that were hidden on some of the devices, and it all comes down to the same place," explained Devon, "The coordinates and the messages that were on the devices speak of the place where X marks the spot. Something is important there, no doubt."

"Great," said Dar, "that was good work."

"But what do we do now?" asked Devon.

"We take it to the council, as always. I will set it up," said Dar.

As Dar departed, one of the techs named Luca said to his team, "While you guys have been taking apart the alien spaceships, I have managed to piece one together."

"No way!" said Devon.

"Yes," said Luca, "come and have a look." The whole team followed Luca up to another level, and there it was, a silver alien spacecraft.

"Does it work?" asked Devon

"It does, but it took me a long time to figure out how."

"Fire it up!" said Devon.

"Just a minute, I have to explain how it works," said Luca. "After much frustration, I finally figured out I needed an alien hand and one of those gloves they wear, that is the key. I made a glove to fit over my hand with the alien hand on the bottom, sort of like two gloves in one. When I managed to get the devices working, it would not recognize my hand, but when I used the alien's hand, it came to life. Look here," he pointed to a small oval screen.

"When I place my hand over the screen, like this—" the spaceship hovered,

"Wow!" said all the techs.

"How do you control the speed?" asked Devon.

"I will not do it here, but to go fast, you tilt the alien's hand forward. To turn it left, you tilt it left. They drive this thing with the palm of their hand, it is incredible. You know, Dar is going to present the information we have on the red X, and he is hoping it gets approved by the council. If we must travel there by horse, that will be a long journey, and I do not know about you, but I am tired of sitting on horses. I say, we tell him about this ship. Maybe we can fly him there, and won't that be a blast?" said Luca excitedly.

Devon asked, "How many can we take on that thing?"

"About five, I would say," replied Luca.

"Okay, let's hold on to this until that time comes," said Devon.

The tech team agreed with Devon's suggestion.

Dar had a meeting with the council. He asked Devon and the techs to join him to help him persuade the council to grant permission to visit the red X. The council said, "Don't you think we have had enough adventure for two lifetimes?"

"Yes," said Dar, "but Devon, Luca and the techs have found some new information the alien spacecraft revealed, and only through their hard work, am I here. I certainly do not want to ride out there for another week's journey of sleeping by fires and bugs crawling everywhere. It is no fun," he said, "but we can get that GOL, who has caused all this trouble, for what he did to us. Let us not forget about Allicin in the archives. Her death needs to be for something."

"It was the GOL," said Lars, "that killed that young girl?"

"Yes, it was," said Dar. "He told me when I had him locked up."

"With that," said the council, "you have our permission to go and check this out."

"Thank you," said Dar, "I must go and prepare for another long journey."

As Dar was heading out of the council chamber doors, Devon and Luca asked, "Can we go with you?"

"Sure," he said, "we will need a small troop with the suits and the swords, you know, same old, same old."

"Can we tell him?" Luca said to Devon.

"Tell me what?" asked Dar.

"Sir, we have something to show you. Come with us." Dar followed Devon and Luca and the techs out of the village hall, figuring they had some new information. The group went to the jailhouse and went to the level where the ship was being kept undercover. They led Dar in and uncovered the ship.

"Wow!" he said. "You guys were not fooling around; you made a spaceship. Boy, I wish we could fly that!" He laughed, "Wouldn't that be great."

"Come on, sir," said Luca, "let me show you around." The stairs were lowered, and Luca slipped on the glove, and he asked Dar to strap himself in. Dar played along until Luca waved his hand over the screen, and the craft lifted off the floor and hovered.

Dar said, "What is this?"

Luca turned to Dar and said, "We got this working. It can fly to the red X."

Dar said, "That's awesome. Can we take it for a ride now?"

"I do not know," said Luca, "we have not flown it yet, but it starts up when we try it."

"We have to try this out," said Dar, "Explain to me how it works."

"Well," said Luca, "I cut off the hand of an alien, because without that, it would not work. I made a glove, to use my hand to guide the alien's hand. In theory, to make it go faster I will have to tilt my hand forward, and to turn it left or right, I tilt my hand left or right. It's amazingly easy."

"When can we go?" asked Dar. "We have to test this thing out."

"Let's open the doors now and give it a rip." So, the techs opened the door to the outside, and Luca slowly placed his hand over the screen and raised it a little. The craft rose a little in response, then it gradually rose out of the lower level. Luca moved his hand forward, and the craft started to go forward.

"Let's go for a little trip," Dar said.

"Where?" said Luca

"Let's go to the mountain and see what's there." So, Luca tilted his hand further, and the craft sped up, and within minutes they were looking at the place where the mountain used to be.

"Where do you want to go now?" asked Luca.

Dar said, "We had better return. I would like to visit the red X, but we need to be prepared for that, so let us return home." Luca shifted his hand, and in no time, they landed safely in the lower level of the jailhouse. Dar and Luca exited the spacecraft and met with Devon and the rest of the team.

"You know," said Dar, "I have to let the council know about this."

"If they say no," explained Devon, "we have to ride horses for a week's journey, but in this, we could be back in a day."

Dar remarked, "A day! You're right. Okay, this is what we will do," explained Dar. "Tomorrow we pack the horses and ride out of town, but we will ride back when it is dark and take this thing. We only need five soldiers, but we must be armoured. On second thought—out of all the aliens that died, did we manage to keep any of their suits?"

"Yes," said Devon, "we have over one hundred of them. We figured there was no sense in destroying them."

"Good man," said Dar, "Luca you will be the driver and also will wear the alien suit along with Devon by your side, just in case, you never know what's on the red X. So, gather your suits, and say nothing about this mission, not even to your wives. We leave at 8:00 am tomorrow, so be ready with your horses for a little trip."

"Okay," they agreed, and left to get prepared for the journey.

The very next morning, the villagers came out to see the soldiers off, and some of the Elds were there also. They shook hands with the members of the council and bid them farewell. Wives and children waved, as Dar said to the horse, "Let's go." And they were off.

They travelled about a mile out of town and dismounted by a river. They rested on the mossy path until evening. When it was just about dark, the team made their way to the back of the jailhouse and gathered their things. Devon and Luca slipped on two alien suits and two more of the soldiers, including Dar, rode in the back of the craft, with their full armour and swords. Luca sat in the cockpit and closed the spaceship's door. He slipped on his glove and placed it over the screen. Immediately, the craft hovered, then he raised his hand, and the craft lifted out of the jailhouse, and they started to fly to the coordinates of the red X. The coordinates were dialled in, and the craft sped there very quickly. In no time at all, they were over the red X.

Then Luca lost control of the spacecraft and said, "We are being guided, I have lost control. The glove does not work!"

"Just go with it," said Dar, as they looked outside. The mountain in front of them revealed a hidden door to a cave, and they were headed for it. "Great," said Dar, "we are going in. Get ready." The craft passed through the cave doors, and they were in a large flat place, but there was nothing else there. Devon and Luca, who were dressed in the alien suits, looked out the front of the craft and could not believe their eyes nor could they contain their excitement, for coming towards them with his hands waving victoriously, was the GOL himself.

"He is coming," said Devon excitedly.

"Who?" asked Dar.

"The GOL is coming our way."

"You and Luca walk down to meet him; I will be right behind you."

"Really, sir, I am a bit scared," said Luca.

"We may not ever get this chance again," said Dar, "so let's get with it, this is it! I will handle it, just get down there."

Luca said, "Come on, Devon, help me out here!"

"Okay, I'm with you," said Devon.

The spacecraft stairs opened by themselves, and Luca and Devon dressed as aliens walked out toward the GOL. He said, "I thought you guys were all dead. I am extremely excited to see you." Then, he backed off when he saw Dar, large as life, walking down the stairs of the craft behind Devon and Luca, with his glowing purple sword in his right hand.

The GOL was in shock and terror at Dar's presence. He immediately drew his sword and said, "At last we meet."

"Yes," replied Dar, "but, this will be the last time."

The GOL stepped back a little way from the spaceship as Dar gently stepped off the spacecraft's stairs and headed towards the Gol with eager intent. They both fought in the middle of the hangar. Devon and Luca stood watching along with the other two soldiers as their swords also glowed. Dar and the GOL's swords were clanging and clanking. The battle went on for over ten minutes, each one delivering a skillful attempt at trying to defeat the other. Dar landed a kick to the side of the Gol that weakened him some, and he gave a loud groan as he felt the blow.

The two of them were getting exhausted from fighting, and they both held a stance facing each other, holding their swords tightly. The GOL said out loudly in his heavy breathing, "You could not leave well enough alone. You had to go searching my private dwelling and stole my book and belongings."

Dar replied, "Your bad deeds have finally caught up with you, and there is no escape this time. Justice is going to be served." With that, Dar moved against the GOL and they began fighting more intensely.

Dar, with an incredible swordsmanship maneuver, managed to sever the GOL's right hand. The GOL felt the excruciating pain as he cried out in defeat, and his sword fell to the floor. The metal sound echoed around the hangar as the sword dropped onto the hard surface, with his hand attached to it at the wrist.

Fully exhausted and breathing heavily, Dar slowly

approached the GOL, who was bent over and kneeling on the hangar floor, clenching his right hand and trying to stop the bleeding.

After he caught his breath, Dar proclaimed, "You're under arrest for the murder of countless thousands, and not to mention my friend, Allicin." Dar ordered Devon and Luca and the two others soldiers who were watching the fight to come and place the GOL in bondage. They managed to find some ropes and other bindings around the giant hangar and tied the GOL up. He was placed securely in the craft, and Luca flew them out of the mountain's entrance but remarked the craft was a little heavy due to the extra weight of the GOL.

Dar said, "When we get home, fly this craft into the middle of the village square." Then Luca slightly tilted his hand and zoomed the craft back over the village in no time. He slowed it down, hovered, and started the descent. It came to rest in the middle of the town square. Immediately Dar could see one hundred or so soldiers at the ready, with red glowing swords circling the alien spacecraft. They were waiting.

When the craft landed, Dar said to the techs, "Open the stairs." He grabbed the GOL and said to him, "You have no idea how long we have waited for this moment. Get out." Dar made him walk first down the stairs. He drew his red glowing sword and walked close behind his prisoner.

The soldiers, the people of the village, and many of the Elds were there. When they saw Dar and who he had arrested, the whole village could not contain themselves. They were all looking in amazement, and gasps of wonderment came from the crowd. Even the Elds were astonished at the sight. The council, Lars and Alban and some of the soldiers greeted Dar as they took the GOL and immediately locked him up.

"First of all," said Lars, "where did you get that ship? We did not know what was happening—we figured we were done for when we saw this alien ship."

"I will explain everything," said Dar, "but we had to keep it a secret, and we acted upon a little info that caught us the big fish, wouldn't you agree?"

"Yes," said Lars.

"Devon, Luca, and the techs are the brains behind this. I was just a passenger; they did all the work."

Devon and Luca plus the other two soldiers who witnessed the fight in the hangar between the GOL and Dar interrupted and said, "Lars, you should have been there as we witnessed Dar take down the much larger GOL. It was simply amazing to watch."

Lars said, "That's why he is our leader. I knew he would come through for us. Do not worry, you and your team will be greatly honoured."

"It's late," said Dar, "and we are beat. But make sure we have plenty of guards on this guy tonight, and we will meet in the morning."

The next day could not come fast enough for the Freed and the whole Solar Complex. Everyone was out to see the GOL on trial. Elds came from everywhere, by the thousands, and the village was bursting at the seams. The time had come, and the council members were ready, along with every soldier, wearing full armour. The GOL was walked from the jailhouse, to be placed in the courthouse in total bondage. Elds piled in the courthouse to see the spectacle. The charges were read, which amounted to the deaths of countless generations of Elds, and the Flawed being mentally tortured with dementia, forgetfulness, and the loss of precious memories of loved ones who had long died before their time. He was also charged with the murder of Allicin in the archives.

"How do you plead?" asked the judge.

The GOL said, "I just wanted it all, and it was rightfully mine." "You had no right to break into my mansion" besides "I have signed contracts to this land"

"Then," the judge said, "You will get what's coming to you today at noon, when you will die by hanging. There is a mountain of evidence and crimes against you. Thanks to the efforts of Dar, the soldiers, and the Elds, we are finally going to be rid of you forever. One more thing—you promised the Elds great fortunes of silver, while they mined for you for years with very little to show for it. Well, where your mansion used to sit—before Dar bombed it to smithereens sits your little treasure of silver. Today, I grant half of that silver to be given to the great nation of the Elds. The other half will be given to the people once called the Flawed, but who now are called the Freed."

The GOL was very hostile towards the judge and shouted obscenities, but great shouts of joy were heard in the courtroom and outside in the village. The judge hammered his gavel one big slam, and the court session ended. The gallows were ready, and the GOL was escorted by Dar, who placed the rope over his head, and then the bottom fell out from under him whose name was called Aldo Baca, but we called him the Giver Of Lies, he died there, in the village of the Freed, in the Solar Complex.

EPILOGUE

SO, THERE I WAS. I OBSERVED, AND I HELPED AS best I could. I stood in the crowd as I witnessed the alien ship come into the midst of our village, and I saw the GOL being escorted by our precious Dar. I witnessed the GOL take his last breath. I was relieved for my family, my friends, and my relatives. I was a little saddened to see the death of another person, but I thought, this was not another person but maybe a devil that came to haunt us years and years ago. All I know is I was happy to see him gone. I was a witness to the carnage of war and fighting, and at times I was very scared. At last, we have peace, and the Darkness has lifted.

The next day, after the dramatic scene in the center of our village, Dar was heading towards the council carrying his armour and full soldier apparel. I got up the nerve, walked up to him and asked, "May I see the soldiers' uniform?"

"Sure," he said, "anything for you Jenny." He laid it down there, in the middle of the town square. He handed me the sword, and I took it in my hand. It felt a little heavy at the handle but not so heavy at the end of the blade. I pretended to swing it here and there. Dar laughed and said, "We are looking for good women soldiers."

I blushed and said, "Really?" Then he handed me the amber. I held it in my hand, it felt smooth to the touch, and all six sides were perfectly squared. "Do you have the book?" I asked him.

"Sure," he said, as he took it out of his vest.

"May I open it?"

"Go ahead." He handed it to me. I turned to the first page, then the second. It was very colourful.

I said to Dar, "The writer of this book must have had a great imagination."

"Yes," said Dar, "it came alive when we had the young ones and when we were at the mountain."

"Yes, I know," said Jenny.

Then he handed me the three keys, and he said, "You might as well see it all, and here is the shield too." I held the keys. I liked the green one best, and the shield was a representation of all the items.

"Can I wear the armoured suit?"

"You don't quit, do you?" said Dar, and I laughed. I tried it on, but it was a little too big for me. But as I stood there with the uniform on, I must admit I felt empowered. As if something was challenging me to go further. I paused for a moment ,it was surreal. I shook my head and came to my senses.

I said to Dar, "from all the action over the past little while, I never saw the uniform up close. I just wanted to see it."

"Any time," said Dar. I slipped off the uniform and handed it back to him. But I remembered the feeling of that suit.

"That was powerful," I said to myself.

Then Abner came strolling past, and he said, "Hello, Dar, it is a great day!"

"Where are you off to now? As if I didn't know," said Dar.

"Going fishing," said Abner, "I have to catch up on a few years. Are you coming, Jenny?"

"Yes, Dad. I will be right there." I thanked Dar for showing me the uniform, then I ran to catch up with my Dad, Abner.

Then Abner sang out to Dar and said "The sky is blue, the grass is green." Abner walked a little further and sang out again, "The flowers are all in full bloom, and best of all, the fish are back in the river and the lakes." Abner sang out again, "Thank you, Dar."

Dar replied to Abner, "Jenny was a great help to us!"

"Thank you, Dar," replied Abner.

As I walked alongside him, I said to myself, "It sure feels good to have my Dad back again."

The End

Acknowledgements

I would like to thank:

- The God of everything who enables me with creativity and imagination.
- My wonderful wife Gail and our three children, Jackson, Abby and Ashton.
- My sister Stephanie for her expertise in designing the cover.
- Christine Driver for editing and David Edelstein for book design.